Black Forest

The
Shades of Hope
Novella Collection

Linda Hughes

In memory of my dad, Robert Lincoln Hughes, Jr.
U.S. Marine Corps, 1941-1945
Known as Bob, Junior, and Red (for his brilliant red hair)

"Wars are started by petty men in positions of power who want more power.
They don't have anything to do with us ordinary people."
Robert Lincoln Hughes, Jr., 1963

"War is stupid. We've got to have love on our planet."
Charles Scheffel, in *WWII in HD – End Game*,
History Channel, 2020

Chapter 1

Unterreichenbach, Schwarzwald (Black Forest), Germany, 1944

Methodically, seductively, the vixen fingered a strap of her lacy white slip, then sloughed her shoulder to release its hold. The thin ribbon dangled down to grace the flawless skin of her lithe upper arm. No longer held taut, the front of that side of the undergarment sagged, teasing to expose a full, bare breast. But the pink berry in the center of that mound caught the delicate fabric and left itself modestly veiled.

He licked his lips.

She swallowed her pride.

Forgoing further preliminaries, she stifled a bored yawn as she released the other strap and let her slip cascade onto the floor. Her exquisite body now naked, she stepped out of the circle of lace and sauntered to the vile man....

Harbor Springs, Michigan, United States of America, 2015

Gertie's eyes flew open as she jerked awake from the nightmare memory, her breath clutching at the back of her throat. She gulped in deep pockets of air.

Nine and a half decades old and still, after all these years, she didn't know how to label her emotions over this. Fear. Sorrow. Sadness. Grief. Humiliation. Anger.

Hatred. That was what she usually settled on. One of those muckety-muck psychoanalysts in the city would have a field day with her, she had no doubt.

Awake now, staring into darkness, the old woman considered her plight. In the morning, her granddaughter and great-granddaughter would visit; reluctantly, obligingly, Gertie suspected; to celebrate her 95th birthday.

Should she tell them her story? Were they ready to hear it? Pfft, they would never be ready to hear it.

Yes, she decided, she had to tell it, had to give her descendants this one opportunity to get to know her, truly know her, before she died. After all, how many years, or days, could she possibly have left on this earth? The time had come for them to know the sacrifices that were made, thank you very much, to bring them the privileged lives they had, lives they mostly took for granted, from what she could tell.

Would they care? Who knew?

Her decrepit, osteoporosis-infested body might be failing, but her mind was not. She remembered every detail of why and how they got to where they were. And she intended to insist that her family members listen to every bit of her extraordinary, lurid tale.

"Hang on to your panties, girls," she whispered into the night, a slight German accent still haunting her voice, even after more than sixty-five years of living in the United States of America. "I'm about to rock your pretty little worlds."

She rolled over on her soft bed in the nursing home. This time she fell into blissful slumber as she dreamt about being a spritely young girl skipping around tall, dark green pine trees in Germany's Black Forest, with nary a care in the world.

Chapter 2

Harbor Springs, 2015

"Did you finish your homework like I told you?" Marilyn's eyes darted away from the road as she drove her Ford Escort down Lake Street in Harbor Springs, Michigan. She glanced at her daughter to try to decipher the sixteen-year-old's demeanor. Kiera sat beside her mother, silently mouthing the words to some head-bopping song. Marilyn tapped her arm.

The teen tugged out the buds, which nowadays seemed to be surgically attached to her ears, and snarked, "What?"

"Homework. Done?"

Kiera cast a Betty-Davis-worthy eyeroll at her mother. "Natch."

Marilyn doubted that, but decided to let it slide for now. They had more important matters to discuss.

The buds automatically headed back toward the teen's ears, as if drawn by a magnet, so Marilyn put out her hand. "Wait. We have something to talk about."

Another eyeroll, this one even more Academy-Award-worthy than the last. "No. Huxton and I are not having sex. I told you."

"It's not that. Although, you won't, will you? You don't need..."

"I know, I know. I don't need to get pregnant and ruin my future. I promise, Mom, my cherry and my future are both intact. For now."

Marilyn caught the mischievous smirk. "Okay. I believe you," she lied, suddenly stricken with how much her daughter sometimes acted like her feisty great-grandmother. She shoved the troublesome comparison aside. "I just, well, I worry is all."

"You worry too much."

"Yeah, well, you would too if you were raising a teenager alone." Her thoughts careened back to her blistering, mudslinging, damned divorce the year before and the fact that at this very moment her ex was sailing off the coast of St. Bart's with his twerpy twenty-three-year-old girlfriend. "Damned bastard," she murmured without realizing it had slipped out aloud.

"Dad." Kiera said it as a statement of fact, not as a query or accusation.

"Oh. Sorry. Listen, forget all that. We need to talk about your great-grandmother."

"I like Granny Gertie. She's cool."

"Yeah, well, Mom says she's been trying to tell some weird stories lately, some very strange things she insists really happened. Her mind is slipping, sliding, gone." She twirled a finger at her temple to emphasize her point. "So don't be surprised or pay any attention to her wild tales. Okay?"

"What if her mind isn't slipping? What if her stories are true?"

"Oh, please. Don't start taking up with the old lady and defending her craziness. That won't help. Your grandmother – my mother and her own daughter, mind you – is even feigning pressing engagements today so she doesn't have to come."

Kiera remained silent, leaving Marilyn to fear her words fell on deaf, bud-encrusted ears.

Chapter 3

"During World War II, I was a prostitute for the Nazis, I murdered my husband, and I was a spy for the German resistance. Your mother's father isn't who she thinks he is."

"Granny! You mustn't say such outlandish things. That's ridiculous."

Marilyn's interruption annoyed Gertie mightily, especially when her granddaughter dismissively patted her arm, stood up, and trounced over to the table with the birthday cake she'd brought.

"How about another piece? This German chocolate cake we made for you at the bakery is de-li-cious!" Marilyn chirped as she plastered fake mirth onto her red lipsticked lips, as if her grandmother hadn't even spoken. She picked up the confection knife and held it in the air, at the ready. But the quiver of her mouth belied her awareness that had been a stupid question, seeing that her grandmother had already devoured two ginormous slices. The old woman had cackled, "What's it gonna do, kill me?" to justify her second helping.

"Put the knife down before I'm tempted to stab you with it." Gertie's frail hands balled into fists and pounded the arms of her over-stuffed easy chair. "Sit down and listen."

"Okay, okay, Granny. No need to get huffy with me." Her face suddenly ashen, even under its perfectly applied layer of make-up, the thirty-eight-year-old carefully put down the sharp utensil and sat back down on the folding chair provided for her visit to her grandmother's room. It didn't escape Gertie's notice that she placed the knife as far away as possible.

"I wanna hear your story, Granny Gertie." Kiera skootched her chair closer to her great-grandmother and gave Gertie's hand a reassuring pat. The child always had been able to steal Gertie's heart, and the young touch to her crepey skin re-energized and calmed her.

"Granny, I don't see why..." Marilyn was nothing if not tenacious.

"I know you don't! So zip it up and listen, and you'll find out why you need to know."

Marilyn frowned and shook her head.

Kiera grinned and nodded.

"I'll start at the beginning. You know I was born in 1920 and raised in a small town, Unterreichenbach, in das Schwarzwald, the Black Forest area of southwestern Germany, near France. It was a beautiful town with hot springs and a spa that attracted visitors. Hills and forest surrounded our little river valley. I loved playing in the forest when I was a girl...." Unaware that her speech had fallen back into the thick accent that belied her native tongue, Gertie's mind took her back to innocently happy times.

Marilyn sighed, already bored. She checked her carefully manicured nails for any miniscule flaws.

Kiera's bright gaze never left her great-grandmother's weathered face.

"I fell in love with Wilhelm when I was fourteen. He was older, a soldier in his twenties. He was so handsome in his uniform! I didn't know yet what kind of soldier he was, or anything about the Nazi party he belonged to. I was a young, naïve, country girl with fairytale fantasies about love. By the time I was fifteen I was married and had my first child, Wilhelm the 2nd."

"And by the time you were twenty-five you had four kids." Marilyn's voice took on the tone of a recalcitrant schoolkid's rote recitation. "The war started. Grandpa was killed. And your first son, too. That Wilhelm the 2nd. Then you and your remaining three kids came to America. Granny, we know all of this."

As her granddaughter rambled on, Gertie's eyes narrowed, her brow furrowed, and her breathing quickened. Kiera didn't miss the animal desire to pounce its prey, but Marilyn blithely carried on.

"I'm sorry for your losses. It must have been terrible. But the past is past. There's no use dwelling on it now." Marilyn abruptly shut up, finally noticing that the grande dame might snuff her out after all.

"You don't know shit from Shinola!" The old woman half rose out of her chair in ire, but her marshmallow backbone forced her to squish back down into her seat.

"Granny, there's a child in the room," Marilyn meekly objected.

"Child? Huh! Kiera, aren't you sixteen?"

"Yes, Granny Gertie."

"Have you ever heard the word 'shit' before?"

"Yes, Granny Gertie."

"There. All settled. I had three children by the time I was your age.

"And if you don't know, 'shit from Shinola' is an old expression from World War II. Shinola was a popular American shoe polish. Great shine on your shoes. Shit, on the other hand... Well, you get the picture.

7

"Now, as I was saying before I was so rudely interrupted, there's a lot more to my story than you know. The past is not the past. If we don't learn from it, it repeats itself. That might be a cliché, but it's true. First of all, I had six children, not four."

Marilyn's eyes widened in disbelief.

Kiera stared in curious wonder, raking her fingers through her long, sandy-colored hair as if clearing her mind. She leaned forward. "Granny Gertie, are you really saying you had six kids, and you were a hooker, and you offed your husband, and you were a spy?"

"You've got it, girlie." Gertie winked and barreled ahead with her story.

Chapter 4

Harbor Springs, 2015

Marilyn nibbled on one of the nails she'd so protectively examined earlier. A nascent speck of red polish unfashionably dotted her front tooth. She looked like a woman unable to pry her eyes off the screen of a terrifying horror movie like *Invasion of the Body Snatchers* or *Night of the Living Dead.*

"My husband Wilhelm was a Nazi," Gertie continued her story. "You hear about them being fanatics for der Führer. Well, the man I once thought I loved turned out to only have love for power and greed and that horrible lunatic, Adolf Hitler. Once I figured that out, we fought about it all the time, until the night he slugged me in the face and told me to shut up. I was smart enough to shut up. By the time the war started, my son Wilhelm the 2nd – I had affectionately nicknamed him 'Zwei', German for 'two' – was no longer my son. He was only six years old when his father turned him over to Hitler's regime to be a boy soldier. He lived in a camp where he was turned into a killer thug. I didn't even recognize my boy anymore."

Gertie's bright blue eyes misted and roamed away from her audience of two to gaze out the window at the lush summertime greenery outside. Lost once again in her dark forest of old, she sighed deeply. When she turned back to look inside, it surprised her to discover others in the room. Clearing her throat, she collected her thoughts.

"It broke my heart. But there was nothing I could do about it. Women had no rights, no say. At least I didn't. I suppose that women married to decent men fared better. But my husband was far from decent. He took all of his cues from the most colossal chauvinist of them all: that damned Führer. Humph. Wilhelm didn't have the balls to think for himself. Das schwein." Her eyes veered away again in horrific memory, then quickly came back.

"The twins came a year after Zwei. Frieda and Friedrich. From the moment they were born, they had a special connection, a bond like no other. She was the strong one, that girl." A smile lit Gertie's face, revealing surprisingly healthy white teeth for a woman her age. "She did everything first. Walk. Talk. Read. Friedrich was no slouch, but he always followed her lead. However, he was… how shall I say it? Okay, I always knew he was gay. It was as if their gender identities got switched in my womb. It didn't matter to me. I loved them with all my heart.

"Their Nazi father did not, however. Right in the middle of their sixth birthday supper, that tyrant showed up and grabbed Friedrich, and started to drag him away. The poor boy hadn't even had a chance to eat a piece of his birthday cake.

Unterreichenbach, 1942

Gerta Gruber laughed joyously at the antics of her twins, Friedrich and Frieda. They had every right to act silly, singing to each other and giggling. It was their sixth birthday. Their mother had fixed them their favorite supper, sauerbraten with spätzle and applesauce. The meat was tough and the noodles thin, but the children didn't mind. She'd knitted them each a set of mittens and caps as presents. New caps plopped on their heads, they sat at the

10

ramshackle kitchen table, happily devouring their special meal while teasing each other.

There had been so precious little to laugh about in recent years that Gerta treasured the moment. War had left them with meager food and nothing for extras like gifts. She'd made their mittens and caps out of yarn she got by pulling apart a knitted shawl of her own.

Thankfully, her two younger children, one and three, were silent in their crib in the bedroom on the other side of the small apartment. Best of all, their father, her dreaded Nazi spouse, was off somewhere making war. Good riddance, as far as Gerta was concerned.

Her kind neighbor had shared enough sugar to make a small birthday cake with a thin layer of creamy white frosting. Gerta adored cooking and baking for her children. The twins tittered with delight when they saw the cake, and couldn't wait to dig in. But their mother, being a good mother, after all, insisted they finish their supper first.

"I'm done!" Frieda announced after taking the last bite to clean her plate. "Cake time!" She hopped out of her chair and did a merry jig.

Gerta clapped her approval. "Very good, my sweet girl!"

Not to be outdone for too long, Friedrich gulped down his final mouthfuls, jumped up, and imitated his sister. "Me, too!" he cheered. The twins grabbed hands and twirled each other around while their mother clapped merrily.

"No son of mine will behave this way."

The sudden interruption of the deep, gruff voice startled all three of them. Experience had taught them to be still and turn their attention to the master of their home.

"Wilhelm." Gerta struggled to control her voice as she stood up, straightened her spine, and wiped her hands on her apron as if trying to fend off their traitorous glee of only moments before. She mustn't further anger this man, that she knew. "We didn't expect you, Wilhelm. Come, sit, eat. You are welcome to what I have left here." She pointed to her own plate.

Wilhelm Gruber stood tall and brooding, his field-grey Wehrmacht soldier's uniform sharply pressed. His wife had no idea who cleaned his clothes these days or where he was most of the time. His dark eyes never left her face as he suddenly swept his arm across the table, sending dishes and food – and the cake – crashing to the floor.

"I don't want your pathetic sauerbraten," he growled. "I want my son." His eyes darted to Friedrich. He may as well have shot the child with his gun, as Friedrich's fear gushed out of him as surely as blood. In the instant it took Gerta to understand Wilhelm's meaning, he grabbed poor Friedrich by the child's skinny arm and hauled him toward the door.

In the many years after that moment, in all the times she'd mulled it over, Gerta could never recall having a conscious thought about what she would do next.

She grabbed a butcher knife and furiously swiped it at her spouse.

It had been a futile gesture, she would always know in retrospect. She'd felt the violent power of his anger many times, but this time it reached new heights, like a bomb exploding. Quickly, as if disarming nothing more than a hissing kitten, he got the knife away from her, grabbed her by the neck of her dress, and raised the weapon to rest its point menacingly at her throat. A trickle of blood slithered down her neck.

Terrified Friedrich cowered in a corner, but feisty Frieda pummeled her father's legs and shrieked at him to let go of her mother. Their faces only inches apart, husband and wife stared at one another in a hatred so palpable, they both would have crumpled in death if looks truly could kill.

Then, without warning, Wilhelm lowered the knife and shoved Gerta to the floor.

"No. I won't kill you. That would make your life too easy." He clutched the knife in one hand and grabbed the boy again with the other hand. "I want you to live knowing that I'm making a real man out of your little sissy here. He will serve the great Führer, as all good German soldiers must. Heil, Hitler!" He thrust his knife-wielding hand up in the ridiculous stiff-armed gesture that glorified the demon dictator.

Before Gerta could scramble to her feet, her husband and child had vanished.

Chapter 5

Marilyn had jumped and Kiera had stared wide-eyed when Gertie gestured wildly to demonstrate how she had attempted to stab her husband to death.

"Yes, my very own husband," she admitted. "I wanted him dead more than I wanted anything else in the world."

The old woman breathed deeply from the telling, her sunken chest heaving as her emotions overwhelmed her. She couldn't speak for many long, measured moments.

"Granny Gertie, let me get you a glass of water." Kiera popped up out of her chair and headed for the sink.

"A beer would be better." Gertie pointed to the small refrigerator by the sink.

"Granny, the doctor says you shouldn't drink," Marilyn reminded her. "How did you even get beer in here, anyway?"

"I have my sources."

"Your heart isn't what it used to be."

The ninety-five-year-old huffed. "Honey, nothing about me is what it used to be."

Marilyn's discomfort intensified as she watched her daughter adeptly open a bottle of Samuel Adams Double Bock, the beer Granny preferred because it reminded her of strong, dark lager, German Doppelbock. Kiera held a glass sideways and slowly poured the frothing liquid. A fleeting thought caused Marilyn to wonder how her teen knew how to expertly pour a glass of beer. She hoped, probably beyond hope she knew, that it was dumb random luck.

"Here you go," Kiera said as she returned and handed over the drink.

"Thank you, dear." Gertie guzzled down a good third of the dark brown brew.

"Let's see. Where was I? Oh, I remember. I tried to kill my husband. That was only the first attempt. I got better at it as time went by." She took another long swig and wiped the foam off her upper lip with the back of her withered hand.

"I thought I would die when Wilhelm took dear, sweet, Friedrich away. I couldn't sleep. I couldn't eat. I could feel his fear and anguish in my heart, and I thought I might die from it. Frieda was the same way, totally inconsolable. She wailed and wailed, like a child lost in the woods. There was nothing I could do to comfort her. Without him, she didn't feel whole."

"Granny, I never even knew you had twins. Why doesn't my mother know? They would have been her brother and sister." Marilyn's suspicion, perhaps hope, that her grandmother was daft tainted her voice. It was easier to imagine all of this to be insane rather than true.

"No, your mother was the last of my children and she came on the boat on the way over here. So she was never even in Germany. You see, I never saw Friedrich again. At first I had no idea what happened to him. I assumed they tried to force him to man guns like so many boys were made to do. Or, more likely, I feared he'd let himself be killed, out of sheer misery. He was no more a killer than I'm a saint. He would have let an enemy soldier kill him right where he stood rather than harm another living being. He was the gentlest soul alive.

"This... this...." Gertie surprised herself by bursting into a torrent of tears. Kiera put a box of tissues on her lap, and it was five minutes before the maven could speak again. She sucked in ragged breaths and said, "This is the first time I've ever told anyone about my darling twins." The look she gave them belied her misery at the memory of the harrowing loss.

"Granny, what happened to Frieda?" Marilyn's tone softened as she finally gave in and started to believe that her forebear's heart-wrenching tale might be true.

Gertie gulped in deep breaths. "She died one month after Friedrich was taken away. She never recovered from the loss of her brother. Once vivacious and loveable, she became sullen and withdrawn. I couldn't do anything to draw her out of it. Then she developed a fever. The town doctor was busy with the troops. I tried everything to make her get better. My neighbor friend tried, too. But in the middle of the night one night, little Frieda simply closed her eyes and never woke up."

Her voice deepened viciously as if she'd been possessed by a recalcitrant spirit. "Wilhelm came home the very night of her funeral. The bastard didn't even know his daughter was dead." She looked off into the distance, transported back to that time by sheer loathing. "We had just buried dear Frieda in the church cemetery and come home, when he drifted into the apartment. I stood in the kitchen, Heinrich and Ingrid playing on the floor beside me. I didn't move. He scowled so cruelly and said," ...Gertie's eyes grew wild with fury... "'Your precious sissy of a son is dead. He died three days ago. Walked right into the line of fire at shooting practice at youth camp. Ah well, he was never going to make a good soldier anyway.' And then he

17

simply walked out the door, as if Friedrich had never mattered." She fluttered her hand wistfully.

Gertie came back to the present and glared at her granddaughter and great-granddaughter. "Friedrich and Frieda had died on the same day."

Marilyn and Kiera did not speak. They stared at the woman sitting in front of them, both realizing they had never truly known her.

"They couldn't live without each other," Kiera whispered.

"Yes. That's the way it was."

They sat in silence for a while as Gertie finished her beer.

"Well, my dears, that was exhausting. I don't think I can talk anymore today. Will you come back tomorrow?"

"Sure. Any time you want." Kiera stood up and kissed her great-grandmother's forehead, and ran a palm along her thick, silky, white hair. "Won't we, Mom?" The teen shot a pleading look at her mother.

"Um, of course. Tomorrow then. Ah, Granny, should we help you get back into bed for a nap?"

"No, thank you. But you can help me into my wheelchair, and take me and my beer out to the patio. I want to sit by myself for a spell and look at the trees. I love the trees. They help me breathe."

Chapter 6

Harbor Springs, 2015

Leona puffed spastically on her cigarette, blowing thick plumes up into the warm early morning air. A blue jay squawked in protest. The seventy-year-old woman looked up into the bird's perch on a fat branch of an old maple tree and quipped, "Give me a break. Okay? I tried to quit. That lasted for a full ten minutes." Unimpressed, the jay squawked again.

"Mom, I thought you quit." Marilyn approached from the path that led into Gertie's lush garden from the house. Carrying a steaming cup of coffee in each hand, she gave one to her mother. "Here you go. A cigarette in one hand and a cup of coffee in the other. That's a perfect start to a good morning for my mom."

"I tried to quit, again. Really, I did," Leona said, responding to her daughter's scolding. "Why did you want to see me out here so early in the morning?" Adeptly, she changed the subject while tossing her smoke into the dirt and using the toe of her wedge sandal to stomp out its cindering tip. Using both hands to cradle her coffee cup, she drank greedily.

Marilyn ignored the question for a moment, instead sipping on her coffee while taking in the spectacular view of Lake Michigan in the not-too-far distance, its vast expanse of deep blue water glistening in the morning sun. Pastel prismed rays of light shot across the sky amongst a scattering of cotton-ball clouds.

Gertie's house sat on a hill seven miles outside the quaint village of Harbor Springs, in the northwestern corner of the lower peninsula of Michigan, where the young mother had settled with her three small children after emigrating from Germany when the war ended. Gertie had been surprised to learn that more than twenty percent of Michiganders claimed German heritage, which helped with the transition. She worked in a restaurant owned by a German couple in Detroit, and after a year they invited her to move to Harbor Springs to serve as cook and baker in a new restaurant they were opening there.

Having always lived surrounded by dense forest, she loved the familiar feeling of security living amongst huge trees, with Michigan's woods hugging the hills around Harbor Springs. And, she immediately became smitten with the new feeling of freedom the openness of the enormous great lake afforded her. Trees and hills on one side; a massive lake on the other side. It had been her heart's home from the moment she set foot there.

After three years, Gertie's baked goods had become so popular in the restaurant that the owners supported her opening a bakery. The rest was history. Granny Gertie's Goodies had been a huge success ever since. The apple strudel was especially popular. Marilyn now ran the business, with Kiera working there after school and on Saturdays.

Incongruously, Gertie's daughter Leona, Marilyn's mother, had always had other plans and presently enjoyed a cushy life with her third in a string of uber wealthy husbands. She liked to joke that she preferred sugar daddies to baking with the real stuff. From late spring through early fall, she and Number Three lived in a lovely renovated historic house in the old-money area on Beach Drive in Harbor Springs. The rest of the year they resided in a gulf-side home of equal grandeur in Florida. They owned an assortment of boats and other toney toys and, naturally, belonged to country clubs and liked to travel the world.

After "the damned divorce," as Marilyn always called it, she and her daughter Kiera lived in a nice apartment provided by Leona. But three months ago when Gertie went into the nursing home, the family matriarch invited her granddaughter and great-granddaughter to "take care of the house" while she was gone. They all knew, however, that Gertie would most likely never be coming back to the charming little cottage on the edge of the woods with her beloved garden and view of Lake Michigan.

Leona stepped up to her daughter's side and joined her in taking in that view. "Well?" she said, getting back to her question about why on this morning she'd been summoned to the home she grew up in.

"You need to come with us today to see Granny. Mom, I'm afraid some of those stories she's telling are true."

Leona didn't respond, instead setting her coffee mug down on a stump and reaching into the pocket of the crisp linen tunic she wore over her leggings to pull out a cigarette and matches. She lit up again. After many long draws, in a practiced move she used the forefinger of her cigarette hand to tap the head of the stick, flicking off its ashes. Then, she stuck it back into her mouth and, without taking the thing out in-between puffs, she quipped, "I was afraid of that."

Chapter 7

Unterreichenbach, 1943

Gerta knelt in prayer, tears coating her cheeks in despair. How could so many Germans rabidly worship Satan himself? That was how she'd come to think of Adolf Hitler, the demon who had stolen two of her sons and a daughter from her. And, yet, her malicious husband still lived. Her mind roiled with confusion. Had the God she'd always known abandoned her? Abandoned Germany? Abandoned Earth altogether? Her silent prayer vaulted these questions at the Lord to whom she had heretofore devoted her life.

Two-year-old Ingrid roused for a moment, and Gerta petted her cheek as the girl lay beside her on the wooden church pew. The child sighed at the touch and fell back into slumber. Gerta gazed down at her, vowing to do everything in her power to keep her and her older brother Heinrich safe from these worries that infested Gerta's mind, every moment of every day. It felt like a snake wound its way tighter and tighter around her brain, making it impossible to think.

Four-year-old Heinrich lay on her other side, blissfully napping. This sanctuary, the Catholic church in town, as much as Gerta presently doubted its purpose, had become a place of solace for her each afternoon. The small, medieval cathedral with its tall, coffered, arched ceiling; and with its intricate, colorful, stained glass windows; provided the only place of peace that existed these days. No one else was ever there.

The priest had given up performing Sunday mass a couple of years earlier, as so few Germans were willing to risk the dangerous taunts and jeers of the Heer, the army land forces branch of the Wehrmacht, Germany's armed forces, who came and went from their village. Prior to the rise of the dictator, over one quarter of all Germans had been Catholic. But those numbers had fallen dramatically out of fear of repercussion.

Der Führer did not support religion, even though he'd been raised Catholic. Now he declared himself to be like Jesus Christ, only better because Jesus hadn't been able to finish his work on earth. Hitler intended to do so, whatever he thought that might be. Gerta had never been able to follow that heretical train of thought, or any of the madman's lines of irrational logic. His rantings had become more and more nonsensical as the years passed, this one especially seeing that Jesus was a Jew and Hitler loathed Jews, blaming them for every problem that had ever befallen Germany.

"Gerta."

She jerked around to see who had whispered her name. She'd been so deep in thought, she hadn't heard anyone else come in. But there was her neighbor sitting behind her: Hedwig.

"Oh, Hedy, you startled me. Guten tag."

"I came to tell you that there have been rats in our building, and I have some highly effective rat poison. I will give it to you." Hedy kept her voice low not in reverence to the sanctity of the place, Gerta suspected, but to keep from being overheard.

Black Forest

Gerta turned to face more squarely the big-boned, forty-year-old woman who had become her best friend. Like herself, Hedy had lost a son to this war. He had been her only child. Sharing the loss of beloved sons, these neighbors had been a source of deep comfort for one another. Hedy's husband, a soldier, had suddenly died of a heart attack a few months earlier.

The women had often held an early morning kaffeklatsch; Gerta and Hedy, and sometimes Hedy's sister Klara; a short time together sitting at Gerta's kitchen table, chatting and drinking their coffee before Gerta's children awoke. As they got to know each other better and trust solidified, they admitted hating Adolf Hitler and the Third Reich, and what it had done to their families. They knew there were plenty of woman who did not feel that way, but they suspected there were many others like themselves who did, other woman who didn't dare publicly, or even privately in most cases, express their beliefs. They heard stories of the Gestapo, the Nazi secret police, being everywhere. Punishment for opposing der Führer was swift, brutal, and final.

Gerta and Hedy figured the Gestapo were too stupid to expect anything of mere hausfraus, so they sat in Gerta's shoddy kitchen and fantasized about escape. Oh, when the war first started in 1939, they hoped Hitler would quickly be defeated and it would all end soon. But by early 1940 they knew it would not be so easy. So, they designed a plan for packing up the children and sneaking into nearby France by traveling through the safety of the Black Forest. When they arrived, they would depend on the generosity of the Catholic church to survive. It was a spectacular, brave plan. They had their satchels secretly packed and planned on heading out as soon as a torrent of spring rain subsided.

Consequently, they were devastated on the day that Hitler's troops marched into Unterreichenbach, their heretofore quiet village, stiff legs and arms making the soldiers look like wooden puppets swishing rainwater this way and that. They set up a transportation base for soldiers and supplies, the town being a waystation on the railroad.

The kaffeklatsch hausfraus' hopes of escape had been washed away.

And it wasn't long before Germany invaded France. The pastoral country surrendered to Nazi Germany on June 22, 1940. Her country was entrenched in what would be a long war, and Gerta, as well as so many others like her, had no place to go and no way to get there.

They had become prisoners in their own land.

Once, after her first three children had been lost to her, Gerta expressed her surprise that Wilhelm sent her any money at all for survival. Hedy reminded her that he would see that as his duty because it supported yet another boy, Heinrich, who could someday join the army. The thought had chilled Gerta to the marrow of her bones.

Now she stared at her friend as they sat in the church. Why here? Why had Hedy followed her here rather than talking to her during their kaffeklatsch?

"Hedy, why are you here telling me about rats? We can talk about that at home."

"Nein. We must not mention it anywhere except within the safety of these walls."

"What are you talking about?"

"Think it over, my friend. Think!"

With that Hedy got up and scurried out of the church like a rodent herself.

Gerta shook her head. It felt like she'd been presented with a puzzle, but couldn't find all the pieces. With thin walls between their small apartments, Hedy knew everything about Gerta and Wilhelm's sordid marriage. She heard the fights. She knew about the horrific way Wilhelm had first taken Zwei, and then Friedrich. She knew that he'd been clueless about his own daughter's death and wouldn't have cared had he known. Hedy also knew that when Wilhelm did show up, Gerta always ended up with ugly bruises and a swollen face.

Her prayers seeming useless anyway, Gerta stood and gathered little Ingrid into her arms, and nudged Heinrich awake. The boy rubbed his sleepy eyes, slid down off the pew to stand up, and reflexively reached for his mother's hand. The instant her boy's soft skin touched her own, a jolt like lightening shot to her brain and annihilated its debilitating vipers.

Ja. There was a rat in her apartment.

She knew what she must do.

Chapter 8

"After that, it was easy," Gertie asserted. "I had no second thoughts, no fear, no hesitation. Wilhelm showed up two weeks later. As much as he'd always derided my cooking, the idiot never failed to eat two big helpings of my apple strudel. I'd been keeping the ingredients on hand. There was a wild apple orchard on the edge of town that the soldiers hadn't found yet, so apples were in ready supply.

"Wilhelm Gruber the 1st keeled over dead one hour after taking his last bite of my delicious apple strudel."

Silence hung in the air as she nonchalantly took a sip of beer and carefully set the glass back down on her TV tray.

Marilyn, Kiera, Leona, and Hank sat mute, staring at her. They crowded around in her room at the nursing home, seated on uncomfortable folding chairs.

Seventy-six-year-old Hank, born Heinrich, had planned to visit the coming week; to see his mother, sister, niece, and grand-niece; like he always did four times a year. After a stellar thirty-five-year career as a pediatrician downstate in Kalamazoo, he and his wife retired near there in the lovely village of South Haven on Lake Michigan. But he was unexpectedly here on this day because his sister Leona had given him a frantic call four hours earlier, insisting that he needed "to hightail his butt up north" to join the clan "right *now*" for a "big reveal!"

"Hank, dear," Gertie continued, "I don't ever want you to feel guilty about me killing your father. I don't harbor one ounce of guilt over it. I did it not only so that he would never turn you over to one of Hitler's youth camps, but because I loathed him. He was a vile man; he needed to be gone from the face of this planet. And, I confess, it was revenge, too, for what he did to your brothers and sister."

Her son blinked, fending off tears. "Mom, I had no idea. None whatsoever. I always thought my father died in the war."

"That was what I wanted you to believe. But now that I'm as old as dirt and not long for this earth, I think the truth is only fair. You are nothing, *nothing*, not one iota, like the monster who was your father. I'm so proud of you, son. When you and your wife discovered you couldn't have children and you decided to be a pediatrician, oh my, I was so pleased that you found a way to help children."

Hank took her hand and squeezed. "I'm a very happy man, Mom. Jessie and I are very happy," he said, alluding to his longtime wife.

"I'm proud of all of you." Gertie looked from one descendant to another.

"Leona, I know I've fussed with you over the years about marrying money – so often – but the truth is, I've liked every one of your husbands. And you know what? It has always given me a sense of security knowing that you're filthy rich. Deep down, I've always known that if I needed anything, anything at all, you'd provide it. I hate to admit that because, as you all know, I like to feel independent. But the truth is, Leona, you've provided financial security for us."

"Well, thanks, Mom." Leona's surprise showed on her face.

30

"And Marilyn. Oh my, you've done such a great job with the bakery. It couldn't be in better hands. You are an excellent baker and an astute businesswoman. Why, you're downright gifted. Don't ever let anybody put you down. Like that ex of yours did. You can do better than that. No offense, Kiera; I know he's your father. But he was never very nice to your mother."

Marilyn beamed and Kiera shrugged, not all that taken with her dad herself.

"And Kiera, dear, you know you've stolen my heart. It's so exciting to think of how you have your whole life ahead of you. I have no doubt, as intelligent and beautiful and wise and fun and strong as you are, it'll be quite the life."

Kiera smiled broadly. "Yup. That's the plan."

"Good girl!" Gertie looked off and added, "Of course, I'm proud of Ingrid, too."

Ingrid, a Catholic nun, had been ministering to poor and sick children with the Sisters of the Holy Mother of Africa for fifty years. Her last visit to see Gertie, her own mother, had been seven years earlier. Clearly, she had long considered her real family to be her God-given African flock. Even as an old woman now, in her seventies like her siblings, Hank and Leona, she refused to give up her work, insisting that it was her life's calling, the Lord's will. Nobody could argue that she was one member of the family who merited their unbridled pride for being a good person.

"We've ended up being quite a marvelously motley crew," Gertie contended. "A family more wonderful than I ever could have imagined. I love every bit of it. I love every one of you."

Proclamations of love were shared all around, and Gertie couldn't have been happier.

31

Chapter 9

"Granny Gertie, what did you do with... you know... *him*?"

Gertie found it amusing that Kiera, the youngest person in the room, was the one who had the guts to ask that question. "Well, I went over and got Hedy, she went and got her sister Klara, who lived three blocks away – we didn't have phones, mind you, because they'd been out for a year – and the three of us rolled him into a rug. Then we drank a horrible coffee substitute that was all we could get those days, and mulled over what to do. It might seem strange, but I trusted those women completely. It was as if some German women had a secret, silent society, an understanding to stick together and help one another. We certainly couldn't depend on our Nazi husbands. In the end, seeing that we didn't have an automobile and there wasn't gasoline to be had even if we did, we decided to pull him on a sled through the forest. It was wintertime and there was plenty of snow. We'd go to the far side of the village, then dump the body behind a bordello there. Whoever found him would think he'd died of a heart attack after a strenuous encounter inside.

"I hadn't even known there was a bordello, but Klara knew all about it. Apparently it cropped up when the soldiers came. It was a good plan. Hedy thought that if I claimed a heart attack at home, it would seem suspicious because she did that with her husband, right next door."

"So, she killed her husband, too?" Hank sounded incredulous.

"Oh, yes. Another rat.

"Now, I'd never left my children alone in that apartment," she continued, "but I had to take a gamble and do it. While you were sound asleep at two in the morning," ...she nodded at Hank, the only one present who would have been there back then... "we schlepped the body in the rug down the stairs, tied it onto Hedy's old sled, and pulled it through the woods. It was a blustery, freezing cold night, so black we could hardly find our way. The name Black Forest had never been more real. It was harrowing work. I was so grateful for Hedy and Klara. There's nothing like getting rid of a body together to form a bond." She couldn't resist a sly grin. "I've thanked God for those women every day since.

"When we got there, we rolled him out of the rug and dumped him behind the bordello. It started to snow hard, so our tracks were covered up. I'm sure he became frozen stiff in no time.

"The plan worked. Two days later a Nazi came to inform me that my husband had been killed in battle. I almost laughed in his face. The lying bastard, sticking up for his comrade. I had to feign grief when it was all I could do not to jump for joy. I must say, I was an awfully good actress in my day." With that she chugged the last of her beer.

"But every bad deed is punished, as they say. Although widows were supposed to get a stipend from the regime, the war was deteriorating for Hitler. There were no checks from the regime. I had to find a way to feed my family."

She caught the glance Leona gave her brother. Hank frowned. Apparently, he had an inkling about what was to come. Leona had filled him in, but like his sister, he probably hadn't wanted to believe it at first.

To lighten the mood, Gertie said, "When I confessed what I'd done to my priest, you know what he said?"

"Nah uh," Kiera answered, rapt with wonder.

"He didn't say anything at first. Then he asked if I got rid of the body someplace where I wouldn't be suspected. When I told him, 'Ja, yes, I did,' he said, 'Good girl. Say three Hail Marys and you are forgiven.'"

Gertie shook her head in disbelief, raised her palms to the sky, and shrugged.

"No way!" Kiera shrieked.

Gertie gave her an affirming nod.

The others, however – Leona, Marilyn, and Hank – had become stricken with paralysis.

"How about we move out to the patio?" Gertie ventured in order to give her offspring a break from these shocking family revelations. "Nobody's ever out there this time of the afternoon. All these old people are taking naps. This room is getting stuffy."

Relief at the suggestion assuaged their shock enough to mobilize them. Hank, still strong for a man in his seventies, picked up his delicate mother as easily as if she were a doll and gently set her in her wheelchair.

"There's a beer for everyone," she announced, pointing at the frig as Hank wheeled her toward the door. "Somebody grab one for me."

Chapter 10

Harbor Springs, 2015

Marilyn sidled up to Leona and put an arm around her shoulders. "Mom, it's okay. We're all here with you. None of this changes how we feel about each other."

Leona tossed her cigarette butt into the dirt, squashed it out, and turned around to fall into an embrace with her daughter. "I know, sweetie. It's all such a shock." She backed away, patted down the front of her blouse as if securing a suit of armor, and acquiesced. "Okay. Let's go get this dog-and-pony show on the road. I want to believe she has a really wild version of old-timer's disease but, even as dramatic as she's always been, I don't think she could be making this stuff up. I have to face the fact that it's true."

They walked around the lilac bush where Leona had sought solace to have a smoke. Gathered around a patio table, the others looked up at them.

"Are you ready, girls?" Gertie asked.

Marilyn took a chair but Leona remained standing, facing her mother. "Mom, if you ki...." She couldn't bring herself to say it. "If... if your husband died before I was born and you had to... had to... work.... Do you know who my father is?"

"Sit down, Leona. Let me start at the beginning of that part of the story."

Leona stiffly lowered herself into a chair.

"Sis," Hank said, reaching across the table to take Leona's hand. "No matter what, you'll always be my baby sister." He smiled so magnificently, Leona couldn't help but nod.

Heartened by the sight of her children together, Gertie said, "That's true. One reason I wanted to tell you this before I die is that I know people are doing DNA testing these days to find out about their heritage. I don't want to leave any unanswered questions after I'm gone, in case any of you do that. We are family, end of story. It doesn't matter who has what father."

Her bright blue eyes sought out the top of the lilac bush as her mind traveled back in time. "Here's how it all happened. By 1944 Hitler's war had been raging on for five years. It was obvious that it wasn't going well. Those of us who were independent-minded enough to see what was happening all along, starting with him taking children in the '30s, you would think we would not have been surprised by anything. But we were shocked to hear rumors; horrible, sickening rumors; about work camps for Jews and other people he didn't like. Those poor people were being slaughtered. It was impossible to believe such terrible things, but it had become clear that the maniac didn't care about anyone but himself. Certainly not for the prisoners, or even for his own civilians like us, either.

"Life for us was chaos. Money became a distant memory. Food was difficult to come by. The troops had stolen every farm animal, garden vegetable, and bottle of beer and wine within miles. Maybe within countries, for all we knew.

"We got ration cards for food. Each card had specific items on it: a reichsfleischkarte for meat; a reichsfettkarte for butter, margarine, and cheese; a reichskarte für

38

marmelade for jam and sugar. Each card had items listed in squares, and the clerk would stamp a square when you got that item. Supplies were very limited.

"The only way for a woman to get more ration cards was to work at the bordello, servicing soldiers. It turned out that Klara had been working there all along. Hedy had tried, but they'd laughed at her, telling her she was too old and too ugly. So, I did it. Hedy babysat while I worked. I paid her by sharing my cards. We shared whatever we had, which still wasn't much, but it was enough to get by. I'm sorry I had to do such disgusting work, but will never be sorry for feeding my children.

Unterreichenbach, 1944

Gerta secured the strap of her slip, making sure it had enough leeway to fall off her shoulder and down her arm, the way lecherous men liked. She missed wearing a garter belt and stockings, but nylon had been impossible to find for years. Barefoot, she padded across the crude wood floor of the old house's attic bedroom and went to the mottled mirror on the wall to slather ruby red lipstick onto her sumptuous lips. Lecherous men liked that, too. From what she could gather, having lipstick on their collars served as a badge of some kind of twisted manhood.

An expected knock came at the door as she smacked her lips to smooth out the color. Thank God this was her last trick of the night. Exhaustion always overcame her after hours of working at this godforsaken job.

"Come in, mein Schatz." The endearment stuck in her craw but, from what she could tell, men were too stupid to know. Fussing with her hair at the mirror, she didn't bother looking up as she heard a man come in behind her and close the door. "Hang your jacket there." Distractedly, she pointed in the direction of a hook on the wall. The jacket came off and was hung up.

Garnering every bit of strength within her, Gerta plastered on her seductive prostitute's lip pout and turned around to face the man. Her pretense crumbled, however, when what she saw startled her.

There stood a Nazi with golden hair and deep blue eyes and a strong body – a perfect specimen of Hitler's notion of Aryan superiority – except that this man looked like an orphaned child. Stooped with fatigue, chiseled features etched with worry, Gerta thought he might collapse right there on the floor.

She stared, speechless.

The man loosened his tie, shucked his shoes, and sunk onto the bed. "I have a favor to ask of you," he rasped. "I need sleep. One hour. I'll pay you well if you'll let me sleep and keep it between us."

She couldn't believe her luck. Get paid for doing nothing but watch a man sleep?

"Of course. Whatever you want."

He toppled over and conked out before she finished the sentence.

Chapter 11

Unterreichenbach, 1944

If anyone would ever have told her she would look forward to going to work as a whore, Gerta would have thought them insane. Yet here she was, tolerating all manner of proclivities with one putrid naked Nazi after another in order to make it to that last treasured hour of the day.

The hour when her friend would come to see her.

Leopold Wolff, a member of the elite secret service, the Schutzstaffel known as the SS, came to Gerta's room every night. That first night he slept like a hibernating bear, exhausted from warring. She hated to wake him up after one hour, but did as asked. As he left, he thanked her and handed over a wad of French francs enclosed in German ration cards.

The Nazi manager of this house got paid up front and instructed his customers to give the women whatever they chose, which usually amounted to a ration card for a loaf of bread or a little money. This man had handed her the equivalent of a fortune.

"Keep some of the francs if you can," he advised. "After the war, our German Reichsmarks will be worthless."

"Danke," she whispered in thanks.

He nodded. "I'll be back tomorrow." With that, he walked out the door.

Stunned at her own reaction – he was a Nazi, after all – Gerta shuddered at the loss of him, placing her hand on the back of the door to try to recapture his essence.

He had suggested that he did not support the war, knowing it was a lost cause, giving her French francs instead of German marks. There was something about him, something so antithetical to her wretched husband, she wondered if he'd ever been a true fascist at all.

Every night for a week it was the same as that first night, except that Gerta garnered the courage to lie down beside him after he fell into deep slumber, careful not to let their bodies touch. She would stay awake, allowing herself to relax and enjoy a blissful rest.

Then one night he wasn't so tired, and they fell into conversation; chatting about their childhoods, the foods they missed, and the movies they'd seen. Anything but war. They even laughed a little. Gerta could not remember the last time she'd laughed like that with a man. He napped a bit before leaving, and then that became their routine.

He asked her to call him Leo, saying it made him feel a bit like a human being again.

She always wore her robe, feeling embarrassed in a scanty slip seeing that the man didn't want sex with her anyway. She knew it was odd for a whore to feel embarrassed, but she did.

The mother did not mention her children. She never mentioned them to anyone here for fear of having them snatched away from her.

Each night he gave her more francs and ration cards. Each night she longed for his presence again after he left.

To her utter surprise and delight, one night he walked in like Napoleon, with one hand stuck into the front of his uniform jacket. With a cock of his head, he pulled out a bottle of wine and rested it on his opposite arm, like a hoity-toity sommelier in a fancy French restaurant. "For you, dear Gerta!"

Not a wine connoisseur, and not able to afford it anyway, Gerta didn't recognize the French brand, but did know it was a Bordeaux that promised to taste divine. "Oh, Leo! How wonderful!" She took the elegant black bottle and caressed it like a priceless relic as she read off the brand name. "Chateau Lafite-Rothschild. It even sounds wonderful." She grinned broadly and held it up in the air with both hands as she twirled around the room in delight.

Chuckling, which etched a long comely line along each side of his mouth, Leo went to her, tossed the bottle onto the bed, and took her in his arms in formal dance posture. Waltzing to imaginary music, he hummed Johann Strauss' *Blue Danube* as they spun around the room. He moved with the grace of a fairytale prince. Indeed, she felt like a storybook princess floating in a dream. Their bodies synchronized perfectly as they pretended to be gliding across the dancefloor of a gilded ballroom to the soothing sounds of a real Viennese orchestra.

Gerta caught herself giggling like a carefree young woman. That pleased him. He stopped humming and stood still, but did not let go of her. "Ah, remember the days when we were free to dance as much as we wanted? There was no fear. No war. It was sublime, wasn't it? Now I realize that we took it for granted. At least, I did."

"I think we all did."

"Ah, ja." Slowly, he moved away from her. Picking up the bottle of wine, he went to his jacket and extracted a wine opener from the pocket. He worked on popping the cork.

"I'll make a promise to you, Gerta." He looked back and forth between her and the bottle. "Someday we will

43

dance to real music in a real ballroom. I will wear a handsome suit instead of this ugly uniform, and a beautiful gown will adorn your exquisite body. We will dance until the sun comes up. Will you do that with me?"

He thought her body exquisite! Her brain froze there and took a few seconds to thaw out enough to catch what else he said. "Why, yes. Yes, I'd love to do that with you."

The cork came out with a *thwup* and, with a playful flare, he tossed the little object aside. "Seeing that we don't have any glasses – I couldn't stuff everything into my jacket, after all – we'll need to drink straight from the bottle. You first, mademoiselle." He handed it to her.

"Danke, monsieur." She took the bottle, sipped, and closed her eyes as the mellow liquid coated her throat with pure ecstasy. "Oh-h-h, Leo. This is so-o-o good." She took two more sips and relinquished it to him.

They sat on the bed taking turns drinking the wine, their backs against the rusty wrought iron headboard, their legs straight out in front of them. As they chatted amicably, Gerta mulled over what was happening here. It was obvious he didn't need to ply her with booze to get her drunk so she'd sleep with him. But she felt certain there had been a connection between them as they danced, their bodies and minds bound together in some kind of magical understanding and concern and, ja, lust. Had only she felt it? Apparently. He'd let go of her. Of course, it struck her, he was not the kind of man who would have sex with a whore.

"Gerta, we really don't know much about each other. I don't want to talk about war. Not tonight. I'm enjoying myself too much. Tell me about your childhood. Were you happy?"

She looked off in memory, then rested her eyes on him again. "I was a very happy girl. My family always lived right here in Unterreichenbach. My father was a carpenter. I was my parents' only child, so I fear I was a bit spoiled. Even though there wasn't much money, I got all the attention a girl could ever want. I know now how very lucky I was. Unfortunately, my parents are both dead, gone for ten years now.

"How about you, Leo? What kind of boy were you?"

He told her about coming from a wealthy manufacturing family but loving the out-of-doors more than business. He'd always felt closer to his nanny, who secretly was his gypsy grandmother, than to his parents. "So, you see, I am a gypsy at heart. What do you think of that?"

She thought nothing could be more perfect.

Chapter 12

Unterreichenbach, 1944

The next night Leo came in troubled, distracted. Restless, he avoided chatting, instead laying down as if to sleep. But Gerta could tell that his mind roiled.

"What is disturbing you, Leo?" She'd never questioned him about the war, knowing that when he was ready, he would tell her about it.

That time had come. "I feel that I can trust you, Gerta. Is that true?"

"Ja. Of course. Completely."

He sat up against the headboard and patted the bed beside him for her to sit. She did,

securing her robe around her body as she settled herself.

Leo stretched out a leg to burrow into his pocket, pulled out a pack of cigarettes and matches, offered her one first, took one himself, and lit them both. Looking at her through the veil of their smoke, he said, "We are going to lose this war. Hitler is a madman. He has destroyed our country in the name of making himself some kind of god. His cruelty knows no bounds." Sadness oozed from Leo's dulcet voice. He inhaled deeply on his cigarette, as if hoping to exhale the horror of it all.

Gerta's mind soared. This Nazi did not support his leader. He hadn't been brainwashed into believing the fanatical bullshit that Hitler endlessly doled out. She'd suspected it, had felt it ever since that first night.

She hadn't discussed Hitler's regime, the Third Reich, with anyone but Hedy and Klara. They dared not breathe a word of their disgust at der Führer because there were still, inconceivably, Hitler supporters everywhere. There was no telling who had irrevocably fallen under his demonic spell or, conversely, who steadfastly remained a thinking person.

"I've heard rumors that his work camps have turned into death camps, where Jews and gypsies and dissenters are worked until they fall over dead," she said by way of responding.

Leo looked at her and for the first time touched her face. Lightly running a finger down her cheek, he said, "It's so much worse than that. Someday the world will know, so I may as well tell you now. He is having prisoners gassed, killed by the millions, and thrown into mass graves like animals. He's trying to eradicate an entire race, and anyone else who doesn't suit his fancy. Including gypsies. If he knew my secret heritage, I'd be dead by now myself.

"Gerta, he is Satan in human form. Do you understand me?"

"Perfectly." Slowly, she took the cigarette from his hand and stubbed out both of their cigarettes in the ashtray on the bedside table. Taking his hand in both of hers, she pressed his palm to her cheek and gazed into his eyes. "He took my first two sons. Child soldiers. I know one is dead, and probably the other, as well. And then he took my daughter, who could not live without her twin brother. I hate Adolf Hitler with every fiber of my being."

"Oh, Gerta." He lowered his hand to take both of hers in both of his. "I am so sorry. How horrible. Oh my God. That monster. I did not know you are a mother."

Proudly, she squared her shoulders and raised her chin. "I have two more children at home."

Black Forest

Gerta watched as awareness dawned on his face. "Ah, I see. That's why you're here. You are making sure your children survive. What about your husband? Where is he?"

"He... he died last year."

"I admire your bravery, Gerta. It must be..." he searched for the right word, but only came up with, "...terrible being here." He gestured to take in the bordello around them.

Having someone besides her two kaffeeklatsch friends acknowledge that she was sacrificing for her family abruptly made her cry. Shoulders slumped, she sobbed into her hands. Leo pulled out a handkerchief from his pocket and helped her dry her tears.

Once she calmed down, she asked a question that had bored into her mind, eating away at her thoughts like a maggot. "Leo, what makes people follow that monster?"

He turned to face her, crisscrossing his legs like a boy and sitting up straight. His answer was thoughtful, measured, and intelligent, meshing with her own suspicions and fears.

After he finished, they smoked in silence for a few minutes, considering the desperation of it all. Then, having made a decision, he said, "I have something to tell you. Something that must remain our secret. You must not breathe a word of it to anyone. Do you promise?"

"I promise." She didn't add that she would do anything for him in order to have him continue to treat her like a decent woman. And to have him touch her cheek again.

Chapter 13

Harbor Springs, 2015

Gertie stroked her own cheek, fondly remembering that night. She'd told her family the main points of her story, the parts that would make a difference to them, but had omitted the name of the man. That would come later. She would continue to leave out, however, the details of her fierce sexual attraction to him. Those memories were for her alone. Besides, her kids weren't dopes. They'd figure that out.

"I'm awfully tired. I'll need to finish my story tomorrow. I guess I needed a nap with all of those old folks in there, after all. Hank, dear, would you please take me back inside?"

"Granny, wait a minute." Marilyn laid a hand on Hank's arm. "We can check you out of here whenever we want. How about you go take your nap, then we pick you up in a couple of hours so you can come back to the cottage for a few nights? Now that we're all together, that would be so nice, don't you think? That way we can relax at home while you finish telling us your story."

"Marilyn, you know the reason I'm here in the first place is because I can't move around by myself anymore. I can't even get in and out of a chair. I need help getting into the bathroom to tinkle, for Pete's sake. I'm the one who decided I needed to be here with 24/7 care. I don't want any of you to have to do it. I'm fine right here."

"I know you are, Granny, but Hank is here to help, and us girls can be your nurses. Come on, come home, at least for a couple of days."

"If I do, where will Hank sleep?"

"He can stay at my house," Leona offered.

"Thanks, Sis, but if Mom comes back to the cottage, I'll stay with her. I can sleep in my old attic bedroom like I did growing up." He gaggled like a nine-year-old.

"There are twin beds in my room," Kiera offered. "Mom can sleep in there with me." She pointed at her mother Marilyn.

"That's right, Granny. Then you can have the master bedroom." Marilyn got up and kissed the top of Gertie's head. "It is your house, after all."

Gertie's face lit up. "How can I resist you children? Okay. I'll come."

"Hey," Leona huffed. "What about me? I wanna come. I get the couch."

They laughed as Hank wheeled his mother back into the nursing home.

Gertie's family went back to the house, her lovely cottage, to prepare for her stay. After a couple of hours, Leona and Marilyn started fixing supper while Hank and Kiera went back to the nursing home to pick her up. After a scrumptious meal of beef stroganoff and brownies with ice cream for dessert, Gertie announced it was her bedtime and summarily retired, with a little help.

The ninety-five-year-old quickly slept like a rock, so everyone else left her in peace and settled themselves in the Adirondack chairs around the fire pit in the garden. Hank and Kiera adroitly stacked wood to build a spirited blaze. A soft breeze rustled the leaves in the trees behind them; the scent of lilac mingled with the smell of burning wood; and on the horizon the sun inched its way to the meeting of water and sky. Lake Michigan dazzled with dancing dots of pink and orange, the sparkling array widening spectacularly as the sun set and sizzled before disappearing altogether.

The clan sipped their after-dinner drinks, a Sam Adams for Hank, Chateau Grand Traverse wine for Leona and Marilyn, and lemonade for Kiera. Leona topped hers off with a cigarette, of course. They refrained from too much chatter as they enjoyed the sunset. Eventually, as the sky darkened and the sparks from the fire wafted upward to join the stars, their conversation inevitably reverted back to their progenitor's shocking story.

"I was six when the war ended and we moved to America," Hank reminisced. "I don't remember much about Germany. I don't think I ever had any concept of real danger. Mom was great. Loving and fun. And, oh-so beautiful. I barely remember the twins. I think I convinced myself they were Hedy's. I do remember Hedy. Ingrid and I adored her. If Mom's goal was to protect us kids, she did a great job.

"When we got on a train and then a boat, and came to a new country, I had an inkling there was an important reason we came. But I didn't know why." He shrugged. "Of course, I've been curious over the years and have researched German history. But this makes me want to study up a lot more on that deplorable Third Reich, to learn more about my own beginnings."

"I'm lucky," Leona said. "I've always known I was born on the boat on the way over here, so I was never in harm's way like you. I never asked her about her life back then, now that I think about it. I always assumed she was a simple German housewife who stayed at home, her husband died in the war, and then she moved here. End of story. Boy, was I wrong."

"I don't think she wanted us to know her story until now." Marilyn stared at the fire, forming her thoughts. "Not that she was embarrassed, but protecting us. Like always."

"She didn't want to break our hearts." Kiera's eyes reflected the light of the fire. "Like her heart was broken."

"Yes, that's it," Hank agreed. The females nodded solemnly.

"I'm glad she's telling us now. I love hearing her talk. In fact...," Kiera pulled her phone out of her pocket and held it up. "I've been recording her. I love her voice so much, I wanted to have it. I had no idea what she had to say. But now I'm so glad I have this. I want to keep it forever."

"You should tell her you're doing that." Hank sounded kind rather than condescending.

"I will. In the morning."

Their thoughts spun, striving to knit together the remnants of everything they had heard.

Hank's voice cracked with emotion. "If she hadn't killed my father, I'd be long dead. As shocking as that is, I know I would never have made it out of Germany alive. I owe her my life twice: first for bringing me into the world and secondly for making sure I got to stay here."

"We haven't heard exactly how I came to be." Leona looked into the night sky, lost in query. "We still don't know if she knows who my father is. I didn't want to believe any of this before. But now I can't help but know it's true. She was one hell of a strong woman to live that life, then sail across an ocean, pregnant with me, headed for a new life she knew nothing about. I can't imagine." She shook her head in disbelief. "I feel like I have no right to ever complain about anything again for the rest of my spoiled life."

"I know what you mean. My damned divorce is nothing compared to what she's been through. To hell with it. I'll be fine. I have Gertie's genes." Marilyn lifted her glass and the others joined in.

"So do I!" Kiera cheered. "I'm proud to be her great-granddaughter."

Leona cocked her head and looked at her brother. "We've lost three siblings. I wonder if they know we survived."

He looked upward, pointing at the starlit sky. "Sis, they're up there, and they know."

They all looked up, pondering the possibilities of what secrets would be revealed in Gertie's story in the morning. They drank up, fortifying themselves for what would come.

Chapter 14

Unterreichenbach, 1944

"**I** will be meeting a man tomorrow night. I'll go downstairs, out back, to have a cigarette. He'll be out there doing the same thing." Leo spoke softly. Gerta's eyes never left his handsome face as they sat facing one another with their legs crossed and their heads bent toward each other like two kids scheming to sneak cookies out of the kitchen in the middle of the night. "If anyone ever asks you about me, you need to lie. I'm so sorry, Gerta, to have to ask you to do this, and I wouldn't if it weren't of the utmost importance. I need you to say nothing about me unless asked. If anyone wants to know about me, tell them we have such good sex that I need a cigarette break. Men often go out back to smoke and relieve themselves. End of story. Can you do that?"

"Ja."

"Danke, Gerta. You are an amazing woman. If this were any other time…" He trailed off, lost in the world of war that consumed his mind like a ravenous monster.

"Are you in danger?"

He sighed, and reached back to retrieve their cigarettes and relight them. He handed one to her. "Ja." He took a deep puff and squinted as the smoke drifted over his eyes. "I am in danger. Many of us are in grave danger. I will not tell you any more than that. I don't want to put you in danger, too. But I think we are safe here. No one thinks anything of a man visiting a lady of the night."

Gerta sucked on her cigarette, pondering his words. "'Lady of the night.' I've not heard that one. I guess that's one way to put it."

"I know you would never be here if you didn't have to be. So many people being forced to do what they don't want to do. Including me. At least we're still alive. Believe me, Gerta, we're the lucky ones."

"My sons and daughter were not so lucky."

Leo took her cigarette and stubbed out both smokes in the ashtray that sat on the shabby bedside table. Then he reached out and hugged Gerta to his chest. She held on for dear life.

When they parted, he cupped her chin in his hand and kissed her so lightly it felt like the wing of a dove dusting her lips. Startled at this turn of events, they sat back and stared at one another. Then, the tacit understanding struck each of them at the very same moment, the knowing that there was no going back. Leo gripped Gerta's shoulders and drew her in for a smoldering kiss.

They made love like ravenous animals, starving creatures whose hunger could not be sated. When they were done, they both lay there staring at the ceiling in a state of shock.

"Gerta… Gerta… Gerta. You have no idea how much resolve it took for me not to make love to you, to ravage you, before this. I may be bone weary and preoccupied with war, but I am a man, after all. But I didn't want you to think me merely another debauched soldier taking advantage of a desperate woman's body. You've suffered too much of that already." Leo rolled onto his side and devoured her face with his deep blue eyes.

"I thought, well, I thought you didn't want me because of what I do here. I'm a prostitute, Leo. Plain and simple. I feel dirty and wicked all the time. I can't stand the thought, it disgusts me so. I certainly understand if a decent man like you can't stand it, either."

He stroked her cheek again. "It pains me to hear you talk like this. We're all whores in this war, forced to do things we would never dream of doing otherwise. You're feeding your children. If anyone deserves a metal for saving lives during this wretched time, it's you. You are so much more than what you do here, and such a beautiful woman. But more than that, you are a good woman, a woman with heart and soul. I said it earlier: if only this were a different time." He rolled onto his back again, put a hand under his head, and looked at the ceiling, wrenched away from her by reality. "But it is not a different time. I have a job to do and I cannot let my desire for you get in the way."

"You're plotting to do something to der Führer, aren't you?" Gerta had guessed it from the moment he'd asked her to keep a secret.

"Ja. He must be stopped."

"You're going to try to kill him, aren't you."

"Ja. It seems impossible, but there are Nazis close enough to him to make that happen, powerful men who also want him extinguished. But such an endeavor takes very careful planning. It is very dangerous."

Gerta put her cheek to Leo's chest, letting her heartbeat meld with his. "Godspeed, my love," she whispered.

"Godspeed to you, too, my love."

Harbor Springs, 2015
Gertie wondered if all ancient people like herself lay awake in the middle of the night fussing about mistakes and

missed opportunities, glowering over successes, and reliving the most romantic moments of their lives. She might be old and withered, but whenever she lost herself in memories of Leopold Wolff, she was young and beautiful and brave again. Her life held hope for endless possibilities in the future.

She sighed into the darkness. Not much future for her now, at least not here on Earth. My oh my, how she would miss those left behind. But the consolation was that Zwei, Friedrich, and Frieda waited for her in the Great Beyond. As a mother, she'd discovered that when a child was conceived, a place in the mother's heart opened up for that child and that child alone. No other child could ever fill that place; each child had their own. So no matter how many children a woman had, there would always be an empty chamber in her heart for the one lost. In her case, there were three empty chambers. The time was close at hand when she could hold her lost children in her arms again and fill that emptiness.

And Leo. He would be there. Would he remember her? Ah, ja. No doubt.

She had loved him so very deeply and completely. With him her longing had finally found a home. He had respected her as a woman – her mind, her heart, her body, her *being*. No other man had ever done that before or since.

The first night that Leo and she ravaged each other's bodies had been the first time she had not used her diaphragm with a man at the bordello. She'd known in an instant that she was pregnant.

In the morning she would tell Leona about her father. She supposed she'd held back for so long so that she could selfishly keep him all to herself, with her most precious memories for herself and herself alone. However, it was time to let go and share the father of her child.

Fluffing her pillow and rolling over, she tried to sleep. But when she closed her eyes, there he was again, that magnificent man to whom she readily relinquished not only her body, but her heart and soul, as well. She might be ninety-five years old, but Gertie wasn't dead yet. Her cheeks flushed and her body tingled at the mere thought of him.

Oh dear, how was that handled in Heaven?

Chapter 15

"Granny Gertie, I hafta tell you something." Kiera set her phone on the table in front of her great-grandmother. "I've been recording your story. I hope you aren't mad at me."

Gertie looked up into the deep blue eyes of the teen, the same color as Leo's, and snickered. "I doubt there is anything in tarnation you could ever do to make me be mad at you."

Kiera's grin showcased the dimples in her cheeks. "That's what I figured. But the grown-ups said I had to tell you. I wanna be able to listen to you when, you know, when I can't hear you anymore."

With that, Gertie laughed raucously. "When I'm *dead*? It's okay, sweetheart, you can say it. I know it's going to happen soon. I'm perfectly okay with that. That's the way it is when you have wonderful people around you and you've lived a long, happy life. Well, for many years now it's been happy."

She looked out at the lake where the morning sunshine showered the vivid blue water with diamonds. They sat in the garden at the table where she and her children, grandchild, and great-grandchild had eaten countless meals outdoors. Now, on this morning, she and Kiera were the only ones left after everyone had eaten breakfast out there. "The grown-ups" had cleared the table and gone inside to get a pitcher of lemonade to quench their thirsts while their matriarch continued her captivating tale.

A vase of freshly cut fuchsia peonies sat in the center of the table. Gertie fingered a velvety petal as she spoke. "What's this I hear about a boyfriend?"

Another grin erupted on the girl's pretty face. "Yeah. His name is Huxton Tanner. My mom's worried because he's twenty-two. He's in college at Michigan State. We met when he was home last summer, and he's home again this summer. He works on his dad's farm. But he's gonna be a history professor someday. He's real smart. And real cute."

"I can well imagine. So, your mom is worried because she thinks he's too old for you? That's only a six-year difference. Not so bad."

"I know! But I think it's the college thing that freaks her out. But, Granny, I graduate next year." She bit her lower lip and sucked in a breath. "If I tell you a secret, you won't tell Mom, will you?"

"Of course not. I'm awfully good at secrets. I'll take it to my grave with me."

Kiera caught the irony and affectionately patted her great-grandmother's arm. "Well, when I'm done with one year of college, he'll be done with his master's degree. We're gonna get married that summer. We have it all planned. I know mom'll say I'm too young to know anything about real love. But I do know. I'm in love."

"I'm sure you are. So, are you asking what I think?"

"Oh, yes. Granny, do you think I'm too young to know what I'm doing?" Her eyebrows knitted together in angst.

Gertie looked at the lake, the lilac bushes, the flowers, the trees, and then settled her sight back on the young woman in front of her. "Well, remember you're talking to a woman who got married at fourteen and had three children by the time she was your age. So, I'm not sure I'm a very good relationship consultant. You know how that marriage ended up."

"Oh, well, yeah. Not so great." Kiera grimaced. "Especially for him."

"That's right. But, be that as it may, I will tell you that I think marriage is a crap shoot no matter what you do. Two people can fall in love when they're fourteen and live in bliss until they're a hundred. And two people can fall in love when they're forty and live in pure misery until they get divorced nine months later. What matters is that you're good people to start with, and I certainly know that you are and can only hope that he is, too. And you need to mature, grow up, together. Commitment is the key. Without that, it will never work. Both people have to be committed. Not the asylum kind of commitment." She tittered at her own joke. "The devotion to each other kind.

"I wish you luck, my dear. I hope you have a lifetime of happiness with this... What was his name?"

"Huxton Tanner. Everybody calls him Hux. He's part Chippewa."

"Oh, I love that name. Huxton Tanner. Is his family close to the tribe?" She alluded to the Chippewa tribe that had resided in the area for centuries, long before white men came. They had a nearby reservation and, recently, casinos, too.

"Ah huh. His great-grandpa was chief for a long time..."

"Here we go!" Marilyn hollered as she came out of the house, carrying a large tray with five festive plastic glasses.

"I've got the lemonade!" Leona followed with a frosty pitcher.

"And I have nothing," Hank quipped as he played caboose.

Once they all settled in, Kiera picked up her phone, hit record, and laid it on the table.

"I adore the thought of you listening to me after I'm *dead*," Gertie teased. "Should I remind you to clean up your room and do your homework while we're at it?"

The teenager fanned a hand of dismissal at the notion. "Nah. My mom's got that covered."

"Mom," Leona said, "don't talk about that. It's so unsettling."

"About what? Dying? If it's unsettling for you, how do you think it is for those of us with one toe in the grave? Ha. Actually, dear, let's face it. It will happen. Sooner rather than later. I'm as ready as I'll ever be. I even believe in God and Heaven more strongly than I ever have before. Hedging my bets, I suppose."

Leona sighed. Hank took his mother's hand and kissed the back of it. Marilyn frowned at the thought of her grandmother being gone. Kiera bent toward her great-grandmother, taking in every moment of her presence.

"Okay, let me get serious by saying that I want you to know that when you've lived a good life, dying isn't scary. I've had more than my share of sorrow, as so many people have during war, but I've also had an amazing amount of joy. You all have brought me more joy than I can ever express.

"But, with that, I'll get back to the sad part of my story. I hope none of you ever experience the despair so many people lived through during that war. I hope that I suffered enough for all of us, and that it's over and done with for this family for many generations to come.

"Now, let's see, where was I?"

Black Forest

"There was a man who asked you to promise to keep a secret," Kiera breathlessly reminded her.

"Oh, yes. The man with the secret...."

Chapter 16

Unterreichenbach, 1944

The next night, the lovemaking was quick, but satisfying all the same. Leo hurriedly dressed afterward, making sure his Nazi uniform appeared to be correct. He checked his watch.

"It's time. I need to go down for a cigarette." He kissed her cheek and left the room.

Gerta threw on her slip and robe, and went to the window. From her room in the attic, she could look down into the backyard. If she wanted, although she did not usually want, she could watch men smoke and piss out there. Seeing that she'd dumped her murdered husband in that very yard, she usually avoided looking. But on this night, she couldn't resist spying on Leo to see who he was meeting. It was so dark, she wasn't sure, but it looked like the top of Leo's head that came into view. It was him. He lit a cigarette, the miniscule spark glowing in the night. Then, out of nowhere, another man stood beside him. He pulled out a cigarette and Leo offered him a light. Two glowing dots moved back and forth as they smoked, like lightening bugs darting about. One of the embers started moving frantically as the man gestured more emphatically. They were arguing perhaps. Or trying to figure out something.

She put on her tattered wool jacket, left her room, padded down the back stairs in her bare feet, ignored the groans seeping out of one of the bedrooms on the second floor, and went down to a side door in the kitchen. It was late. Lights were out. No one was about. She cracked the door and listened. Silence. She slipped out and tiptoed to the back corner of the house, the evening dew on the grass sending a shiver from the bottom of her bare feet all the way up her spine to the base of her skull. She shook it off. From this vantage point, she could hear the men talking in strained low tones.

Remaining hidden, she eavesdropped until she could no longer remain silent.

"I want to help," she insisted in a soft voice as she stepped out of the shadows.

"Gerta," Leo hissed. "Go back inside. There is nothing you can do here."

"I can. I can do it."

"Nein. Absolutely not. Go back upstairs."

She wrestled between her loyalty to this man she loved and her loyalty to herself. "Nein."

Her lover stared at her in disbelief.

The other Nazi calmly smoked and studied Gerta. "I think that's an excellent idea. No one will ever suspect a woman like this."

She ignored him and addressed Leo. "My friend will come with me. No one will ever suspect two women 'like this.'"

"Gerta," Leo insisted, "You must go back inside. I'll be up in a minute. Go *now*."

She slid into the dark and retraced her steps. Leo came into her room five minutes later.

Running a hand through his thick blond hair, anguish contorted his features. His voice conspiratorially low, he said, "Nein, Gerta. I cannot allow it. You have children."

"He stole three of my children. Please don't try to stop me from doing this."

Leo grabbed her by the shoulders and stared her down, his eyes wild with fear. "You don't know how dangerous this is. You must stay out of it."

"Nein." He let go of her and backed away, as if looking at a stranger. "You said yourself that it must be done," she reminded him. "Der Führer must be eliminated. It's a matter of patriotism. If we truly love Germany, this is the only way to save its people.

"I can deliver the payment and get the package you so urgently need. Is it a bomb? Never mind, I know you won't tell me. But that would be smart. Getting a part or having the explosive made out here in the middle of nowhere, away from Nazi headquarters in Munich and away from Wolfsschanze, his Wolf's Lair, and Berghof, too, the fancy home in the Alps he shares with his mistress, that Eva Braun. You'd be more likely to get caught making a device near him.

"I heard you and that man down there," she said, pointing to the yard, "say you two were slated to do this, but now you've been called back to Munich early tomorrow morning. It must be done tomorrow. Your comrade is right. No one will suspect me and my friend Klara. We'll be two stupid hausfraus going to the appointed shop on some pretense.

"If you don't let me do it, I'll go to him." She pointed to the yard again. An insatiable need had overtaken her senses. She had to do this. Without it she would spend the rest of her life feeling like a coward. "I heard him tell you where he is staying. He will tell me what to do."

Leo dragged his tortured eyes away from her as his body fell in on itself in defeat and slumped onto the side of the bed. "Oh, Gerta, I never would have come here if I'd known this would happen."

"But you did come and it has happened. I must do this, Leo. I must, for my children, the children of Germany, and the children of the world."

The look of sorrow he shot her way made her want to weep. But weep she would not. There was work to do.

Slowly, reluctantly, Leo unbuttoned the flap over the breast pocket of his uniform. "I didn't trust leaving this in my quarters. Give this to the man." He handed Gerta a large wad of francs, British pounds, and American dollars. "Be as secret about it as possible. I doubt anyone will be watching, but be careful anyway. Hide it inside something you hand to him."

"Leo, where do you get all this money?" Her eyes bulged in consternation.

He huffed disgustedly. "It's easy. Some German soldiers steal everything they run across. The Jews in concentration camps have been robbed blind. All I have to do is go to the safe in the officers' headquarters and take a handful, like many other officers do. Banks had cash from different countries stashed away. Now it all belongs to the Third Reich. I know it's stolen from innocent people. But they are never going to get it back. It may as well be used for good.

"Here's yours." He pulled out a smaller bundle, like usual, and then a second one like it, and handed them to her. "You will earn it well. You are the bravest woman I've ever known."

Solemnly, he gave her instructions for her mission the next day. She solemnly committed them to memory as he made her repeat every word.

Then they made love again, this time so tenderly Gerta felt as if she floated between Heaven and Earth, never to return to the destitution of her life. There was an urgency in their coupling, a yearning so sweet it etched itself into her soul, lest it be stolen away.

"Gerta," he moaned softly into her ear, "I love you, Gerta. I want you forever and always."

"I love you, too, Leo. I *am* yours forever and always."

As he dressed, he pulled something from his pocket, concealing it in his fist. He held out his hand and opened it to reveal a lovely old ring with a small sapphire surrounded by diamond chips. "It was my grandmother's, the gypsy's. Will you marry me, Gerta? As soon as I return from Munich?"

She flew into his arms. "Of course I will!"

Shortly after, the pain of their parting so overpowered her, it felt as if the hand of the dictator himself reached inside her chest and tore out her heart. Leo did not know when he would be able to return. This time when the door closed behind him, she crumbled to the floor, and pressed her cheek and palms to the cold door. She kissed the ring on her finger, and sobbed.

Chapter 17

"So," Leona said. "Leopold. Leona. I'm named after that man. He's my father, isn't he?"

Once again, Gertie left out the details about making love to Leo, but she knew the kids got the picture.

"Yes. I'm sure of it."

"It couldn't be any of the other men you were with?"

"No. I was fastidious about using protection. He was the only one I didn't use it with."

"That means I'm not a Gruber like Hank and Ingrid. I'm a… Wolff, you said?"

"Yes, that's it."

Leona stared at her mother. "Wow. I'm a Wolff. And… and I'm part gypsy?"

"Yes. All of you girls are." Gertie pointed from Leona to Marilyn to Kiera. "He told me the story of his grandfather falling in love with a beautiful, dark-haired Romanian gypsy. Romani they were called. It was such a scandal that his father made up a story about him having been married, his wife having had a baby and dying in childbirth, and this foreign woman being hired as the nanny. That way, Leo's grandfather and his gypsy lover actually lived together for the rest of their lives, raising their son, Leo's dad. Then she became Leo's nanny, too. He adored her."

"A gypsy!" Hank bellowed and jovially slapped the table. "Of course. That explains your life perfectly, Sis."

Leona puckishly swatted her brother's arm. "Oh, you," she chided.

"So, I'm part gypsy, too. Cool." Kiera wiggled happily in her chair.

"Well, I don't feel like a gypsy at all." Marilyn, ever the practical one, bemoaned the absence of any hint of a wild spirit in her blood.

"I have some things for you girls. Things from Leo. Kiera, dear, would you please run inside and get that small leather satchel I left on the dining room table?"

"Sure." The girl hopped up and jogged inside, quickly returning with the bag.

Gertie handed it to Leona. Leona's eyes narrowed in confusion as she opened it and peered inside. "Francs. French francs. And...." She pulled out the money and a yellowed card. "It's in German. What does it say, Mom?"

"It's a ration card for three loaves of bread."

"He gave these to you. And you kept them all these years."

"Yes. Children, I must tell you that he was the love of my life, my kindred spirit, my one and only, my soulmate. Whatever you want to call it, he was it.

"Oh, after moving here I dated others every now and then. It's not like I tried to become a born again virgin or anything. There were even a few marriage proposals over the years. But no one could ever measure up to Leo. He was the most brave and moral and compassionate person I've ever known. Once you've been in love like that, and been bound by fear and hope, and worked on a secret mission that could change history, all at the same time, nothing else can compare. Every other man is as bland as milquetoast after that."

"Mom, what was your secret mission? Were you in danger?" Hank asked.

"Ah, well…"

Unterreichenbach, 1944

Gerta and Klara trekked to the town center to visit Herr Schmidt's Repair Shop. Gerta had always loved the village she'd lived in all her life, nestled into a valley in the Black Forest. The quaint shop-and-café-lined center of town, the cozy hotels and spas that were so popular with tourists, the clear Nagold River, the old timber mills, churches with towering steeples, and the Alpine train station that could carry one north into Germany or south into France: it had seemed the perfect place to live, especially on a day like this when vivid fall colors emblazoned the hills surrounding them.

Now that Nazi soldiers had invaded, however, there was no dawdling or casual strolling for women, no taking time to enjoy the ambiance of their beloved hometown. Too often they were taunted with soldiers' ribald comments or gestures as they stood in line at the bakery or butcher shop, or as they merely walked down the street.

Gerta and Klara soon reached the shop. It looked different from the last time Gerta had been there, now stuffed to the rafters with military equipment in need of repair.

Gerta had a metal meat grinder in desperate need of fixing. Grinders like that were invaluable with meat so hard to come by. A grinder allowed a hausfrau to mix breadcrumbs or stale crackers into her meat to make it feed more hungry mouths. But the handle of this one had fallen right off. Never mind that she and Hedy had to hammer the thing to death to get it apart.

Hedy stayed behind in the apartment with Heinrich and Ingrid, with strict instructions about what to do should her friend and her sister mysteriously never return. Gerta had given her a shoebox full of francs and ration cards in case of that emergency.

"Herr Schmidt, guten tag," Gerta greeted the wizened old man.

"Guten tag, Gerta. And it's Klara, isn't it?" Klara nodded agreeably. "What can I do for you fine ladies today?"

Gerta handed over the grinder, which was wrapped in old newspaper. "My meat grinder broke. I'm sorry to say I have no money to pay you, but I'll be going out to the orchard tomorrow, and can bring back a nice bucket of apples for you."

"Oh, that would be wonderful." He took the package and when he unwrapped it, his eyes widened ever so slightly at the sight of the roll of money inside. Adeptly, he turned the grinder upside down to hide the contraband and studied the handle that had broken off. Gerta could tell he'd been surprised it was she who'd delivered his payment, but he didn't let that flummox him.

"Let's see," he mused, stifling a chuckle at the sight of the manipulated damage. "This won't take long. Can you come back in twenty minutes?"

Gerta looked down to see that the roll of money had disappeared with the sleight of hand of a magician.

The two neophyte spies hurriedly walked to the edge of town as rainclouds gathered overhead. Ignoring a soldier's whistle as they passed, they could finally relax and slow down upon reaching a path that led along the river. They chatted inanely as they strolled, trying to sound as nonchalant as possible. Gerta forbid herself to look behind to see if they were being followed. That would be too conspicuous.

The path was lovely on this fall day, even in the gloom of grey clouds overhead. Large pine trees left a carpet of fallen needles along the way, providing a cushion like a thick Persian rug. Colorful falling leaves cast themselves about. Gerta hadn't been there in ages, and wished she could enjoy the sojourn, recalling days past when she'd delighted at being there.

Twenty minutes later, they were back at the shop, picking up the "grinder," which was now packed in a small wooden box, nailed shut. "I don't want it to get wet," Herr Schmidt explained. "It looks like rain any minute now."

"Danke, Herr." Gerta thanked the man and both women waved back at him as they left the shop. Once outside, they gazed up at the sky. Clouds became angrier by the minute. Without a word, they scurried along to their next destination.

Chapter 18

Unterreichenbach, 1944

There were many paths from the village into the Black Forest. For eons people had foraged the woods for firewood and building supplies. Pine, spruce, oak, elm, and other trees abounded. Mushrooms and berries thrived as well, providing that sustenance for the villagers.

Gerta and Klara took the path that would lead them to the person who would relieve them of their package. Having no idea who that might be, they felt trepidatious and curious at the same time.

As they swiftly walked in silence, Gerta became truly afraid for the first time. What if the plan had been intercepted and the Gestapo, the secret police, awaited them? What if she never got to see her children again? How could she have put herself and her children in such danger? Leo had been right! The urge to run overwhelmed her. She ought not to have done this. She'd thought herself a brave woman. Perhaps she was no more than a stupid idealist after all. Even as the clouds scattered and the sun broke through to cast down warm rays, her heart raced and she broke out into a cold sweat.

"Ah, der waschlappen," Klara mumbled, her own fright slipping out as she called her friend a wimpy dishrag. "You're as pale as a verdammt ghost. Here, give me the box."

Gerta gladly handed it over and unbuttoned her jacket to cool down.

But when Klara tripped on an exposed tree trunk, Gerta grabbed back the box. "Shaisa!" she swore. "Don't drop it! It might go off."

Now Klara's pallor matched Gerta's.

It took forty minutes to reach their destination, the intersection of their path with a two-lane dirt road. No one was there. They stretched their necks to look all around. Nein. No one. They waited. And waited. Now they both looked like wimpy dishrags, with nervous sweat coating their brows.

The breeze rustled the trees. Red and orange and brown leaves pirouetted in the air as they floated down to the ground. The keen smell of fall heightened Gerta's senses.

Then she heard it, the distinct hum of an engine coming toward them. A sleek, shiny, black automobile crested the hill.

"Oh mein Gott, it's the mayor, Herr Hoffman. That's his 1939 Mercedes Benz. I know that because Wilhelm always lusted after that car whenever we saw it in town. He'd go on and on about it. I haven't seen that car or the mayor and his wife in a year or two."

"Shaisa," Klara groaned. "I've heard rumors that they come out here for some hanky-panky in the woods. What if he isn't our contact and he messes up the whole plan?"

"Act normal. We have to stay calm."

"This isn't normal and we're not calm."

"Pretend."

The classy vehicle, elegant chrome trim gleaming in the sudden sunlight, came to a halt. The mayor – a handsome, square-jawed man of about forty – waved out his open window. "Guten tag," he greeted them. "What a nice day for a walk in the woods, eh?"

The two novice spies didn't have time to respond before the mayor's petite, glamorous wife got out of the passenger side and smiled warmly. "Ja, what a good day for a walk. I remember you two. Gerta and Klara, isn't it? We've met at a few town festivals. Before the war, of course."

Even though Gerta had indeed met the stunning woman before, she was so struck by her sophistication, she couldn't help but stare. The woman's dark hair was perfectly coifed in fancy finger waves. Where did someone get a silky dress, fancy plaid wool jacket, and cute cocked hat like that? And nylon stockings! With pumps, no less.

Gerta hadn't seen clothes like that since the late 1930s and wouldn't have had the money to buy them if she had. She'd worn the same two dirndl skirts, three blouses, and one housedress for five years. The threadbare coat she wore was the only one she owned. She wore her one pair of shoes, ugly black flats, everywhere. The slip and robe she wore at the bordello belonged to the establishment, not her. Even lipstick came compliments of the house of ill repute. She did own one felt hat, riddled with moth holes, that she wore to church every Easter Sunday.

Klara found her tongue first. "Why, Frau Hoffman, how good of you to remember."

"Ja," Gerta agreed. "It's good to see you again."

"Oh, please," the woman fluttered a lovely hand. "Call me Katrin. Here, let me relieve you of that clumsy package." She took the box out of Gerta's hands as if handling nothing more than an empty sack. Her husband got out and opened the trunk, she placed the mystery package inside, and he closed the trunk, swiping his hands together to indicate job done. Gerta suddenly understood that it would have been too dangerous for them to be connected to Herr Schmidt, thus this transfer.

"Auf wiedersehen, ladies. Enjoy the rest of your walk." The mayor dipped his chin and put two fingers up to his fedora in a gentleman's salute of respect, and returned to his vehicle.

Katrin Hoffman however, reached into the pocket of her chic jacket, and for one terrifying moment Gerta feared they'd been found out and the woman had a gun to shoot them dead. The hausfrau panicked and her heart stopped altogether as the socialite maddeningly rummaged for something in that pocket. In agonizing slow motion, Katrin Hoffman withdrew her hand and held it out.

"Danke, Gerta. Danke." A wad of cash slipped into Gerta's hand.

The mayor's high-class wife returned to their high-class vehicle. It backed into the woods to turn around, fall leaves crunching under its snazzy wheels, and left the way it had come.

Gerta and Klara gaped at the wake of road dust that was all that remained of the traitors, as if they'd been nothing more than a ghostly apparition.

Chapter 19

"Wow, Mom." Hank whistled in wonder. "I've heard there were attempts on Hitler's life, but never in a million years did I think my own mother had something to do with one of them. You were so brave!"

"Mom, what happened to my father?" Leona asked, fixated on that part of the story.

Gertie knew that her daughter had a right to know, but this telling would be one of the most difficult of all. She'd managed to talk about her lost children. Could she go through this one more time? Yes, she decided, because there might not be another time.

The whole family still sat at the table in the garden. The lemonade pitcher had been drunk dry, and the summer sun had angled its way around to turn Lake Michigan a bright blue. They sat in the shade and Gertie, once again along with hundreds of other times, thought this the loveliest spot on Earth. It gave her strength.

"It was a week before I knew what had happened to Leo. I stopped going to the bordello. I had plenty of money and ration cards by then. He knew where I lived. Each day I expected a knock at the door. Each night I would lay awake straining to hear that sound.

"After a week, I took you kids …" She pointed at Hank. "… to the church one afternoon. Even though I got down on my knees on the prayer bench, I didn't really pray anymore.

I'd given up. But I still loved the peacefulness of the place. I knew that when he came, Leo would wait for me at the apartment if I wasn't there. I had total faith in him. I knew he would come.

"Then, while I was kneeling there with you children sleeping on the pew by my side, I heard someone open the door at the back of the church." Lost now in her memory, Gertie gestured as if opening a door. "That big old carved wood door made the loveliest creaking sound when you opened it, the sound of having been opened thousands of times by thousands of people over the years. It was usually reassuring, knowing that so many others had found solace and hope in this place. But it was not reassuring on that day.

"I didn't turn to look. Somehow I knew, deep in my gut, who it was. It was as if a moribund feeling I'd buried for days burrowed up and stared me down, like a skeleton clawing its way out of its grave. The soft footfalls down the aisle of the church confirmed it."

Unterreichenbach, 1944

Katrin Hoffman sidled into the pew and sat down. She lifted a white gloved hand as if to touch sleeping Ingrid's angel white hair, then thought better of it.

"You have beautiful children, Gerta. You are a wonderful mother to do for them what you have done."

Gerta didn't take her eyes off of the ornate statue of the Virgin Mary ensconced in the wall in front of their row of pews. Tears gathered in her blue eyes, and she could have sworn she saw some there in the Virgin Mother's brown eyes, too, as the Madonna's outstretched hand reached out to her.

Katrin paused before saying, "You know why I have come."

"Ja."

Neither of them spoke for long moments, as if waiting for the holy statue to provide a miracle and deliver them from the hell of their misery. But, alas, the miracle did not come.

"Leo is gone." Katrin finally said it, her voice catching on the last word as a sob escaped her quavering lips.

Gerta could not speak. She cast her eyes to the floor and tried to breathe. When she turned to look at Katrin, her words faltered. "D-did, did the plan work? Is der Führer dead?"

The distress etched into Katrin's face would have saved her from answering, but she said, "Unfortunately, no. The bomb was planted as planned, but at the last minute der Führer moved to another room because that room was too warm. The bomb went off and only killed one office worker. A damned warm room foiled our plot." She paused again, agony straining her ability to go on. Eventually, she continued. "Leo's death had nothing to do with that. Hitler had him executed the day after he arrived in Munich." She hesitated again, searching for the right words. "If there is any comfort at all in this horrible news, it is in knowing that he was guillotined, along with other officers. It was a quick death. We're hearing of brutal, monstrous torture for some. Thank God he was spared that."

Silence pressed in as both women looked up again at the statue of the Virgin Mary.

"But we're certain," Katrin continued, "that der Führer and the SS know nothing about us. You and your family, and the rest of us here, are safe. You see, Leo was originally called back to Munich on official SS business. Unfortunately, he had coffee with his cousin, a man he's known all of his life. We do not believe that Leo would in any way have shared our plan with this man. But both men were arrested and executed the next morning. The cousin had been deemed a traitor for some reason we don't know and Leo, only because they sat together over coffee in a café, was accused of being a traitor, as well. There was no evidence whatsoever against Leo, but that doesn't matter anymore. There are no trials, no juries. Only our mad dictator's accusations, convictions, and sentences. He's become so paranoid he's killing off his own men, many who are innocent of betrayal. Their true crime, however, is having been loyal to Hitler."

Katrin became still, gazing again at the statue on the wall. "I think the Virgin Mother understands your pain, Gerta. You both have suffered so much loss." With that the kind woman stood, pressed a hand to Gerta's shoulder, and said, "Would you like me to help you take the children home?"

"Nein, danke. I'd like to be here alone with them for a while longer."

"I understand." Katrin Hoffman quietly walked away. When the creaking door closed behind her, Gerta suddenly became suffocated by loss. Her Leo was gone. He'd so infused himself into her being it felt as if she had died, as well. Never to hear his voice again, or feel his touch, or make love with him – impossible. How could life go on without him by her side when he was part of her?

That compounded the holes in heart, endlessly yearning for her lost children. Never to hear their voices again, either, never to feel their touch again....

Every bit of hope, every dream she'd ever dared to conjure, every ounce of peace and joy she'd ever known – all of it evaporated into thin air. Empty, bereft, and hopeless, it seemed there was no way for her to find so much as a sliver of happiness for herself or her children in this crazy, cruel world. She twisted the precious sapphire ring on her finger, and wept.

"Mutter, why are you crying?" little Heinrich asked as he sat up and rubbed his sleepy eyes. Impulsively, he leapt into his mother's arms and ran his small hands down her cheeks to wipe away her tears. "I love you, Mutter. You don't have to cry." He flung his arms around her neck and squeezed.

Ingrid stirred and clasped onto her mother's side. "Me, twoo," she lisped.

Gerta looked at the Virgin Mary again. Did the holy mother look down right at her? Did her raised hand offer consolation and strength?

The mother had no idea.

She trudged home holding the hand of a child on each side of her, knowing that there was another between them in her belly. Her life might be over, but her children's were not. For that, she must carry on.

Chapter 20

Gertie peered up to see her children staring gape-mouthed at her. All of them: her son Hank, daughter Leona, granddaughter Marilyn, and great-granddaughter Kiera.

"Well, I guess you know the rest of the story. The war ended, that coward Führer took the easy way out, and my priest asked if I wanted to bring my family to America. I didn't know what laid ahead for us, but I sure as hell didn't like what was behind us, so figured I didn't have anything to lose. Hank, you were six, as you know. Ingrid was four. A nun traveled with us. She was on her way to work at the parish in Detroit, and she helped a lot with you children, especially Ingrid. I'd never been on a boat in my life, so on top of morning sickness like none I'd ever experienced before, I was seasick the whole way."

"I'm sorry, Mom," Leona apologized.

"That's okay. We all made it.

"It seemed that from the moment the sister took my little girl's hand, Ingrid's fate was sealed. She never wanted to be anything other than a nun.

"The sister confessed to me on the boat on the way over that the Hoffmans paid our passage and gave her money to make sure we got settled. The Catholic church was helping immigrants, too, so the transition was easier for us than for most.

"And, of course, I had all that money from Leo. For a long time, I squirreled most of it away, but once I started making good money at the bakery and felt secure here, I knew I could take care of you kids. I even started buying the property and rental houses you know about in town, the ones my lawyer takes care of, and that's all going to go to you." She gestured to indicate all of them. "So I donated Leo's money to Jewish children's charities. It was almost $73,000. I never felt like it was mine, knowing it had been stolen from innocent people. Leo was right: they were never going to get it back, but at least by donating it I felt like it went to a more rightful place. I think Leo would have done the same thing.

"So many people helped us here; the church, the owners of the restaurant, townsfolk; from the very beginning, we never needed that extra cash, anyway. After the oppression of living under Hitler's regime for so many years, it was such a relief to once again know there truly are so many good people in the world.

"I missed my friends Hedy and Klara something awful, and we wrote back and forth for the rest of their lives. Both seemed content enough, eventually, and that made me glad. They've both been gone for many years now.

"We'd been in Detroit for a year when I was invited to move here to Harbor Springs to work." She swept her hand in the direction of town. "I was happy to move to a village so much like the one I grew up in. Both towns are about the same size. Both are in beautiful settings. Both attract tourists. Both are removed from big city life. I knew this was for me and my family.

"And here we are. Sitting in the loveliest place on Earth, my garden, surrounded by love.

"My life is fulfilled.

"Now, who's going to help me into my wheelchair so I can go inside to pee?"

She chuckled at once again having bowled over her offspring.

After a long afternoon nap, and then a fantastic supper of wiener schnitzel, au gratin potatoes, Brussels sprouts, sourdough rolls, and peach cobbler, Gertie felt spryer than she had in a long time. She even used her cane to move herself from her wheelchair to the sofa. She was staring at the patterns made by the rain dribbling on the window outside, when Kiera came in with a young man.

"Granny, this is Hux."

He had a distinctly striking face and jet black hair. Earthy, strong, alluring. Those were the descriptions that popped into Gertie's mind.

Kiera stood beside him, beaming. The sexual attraction between the two young adults smoldered right below the surface, like sparks under kindling ready to burst into flames.

"Hello, Mrs. Gruber," he offered, holding out his hand. His smile proved the old saying "he lit up a room" to be spot on accurate.

Gertie took his hand but rather than shake, she let her palm rest in his for a moment. He had rugged hands, farmer's son's hands. "The pleasure is mine. And, please, call me Granny Gertie. Everybody does. You know, with the bakery and all those 'goodies.'"

"Oh, yes, I know. My whole family loves your bakery. In fact, about once a week my mom drives all the way around the bay from our farm outside of Petoskey for your cinnamon twists. She wouldn't dare come home without a dozen."

That smile again. Gertie could see why her great-granddaughter was smitten.

"Here," she said, "sit down beside me." She patted the cushion on the couch next to her. He sat down and before Kiera had a chance to plop down on the other side of him, Gertie said, "Honey, why don't you go get your friend a beer. That way I won't have to drink alone." She picked up her glass from the side table and took a sip to emphasize her point.

"Sure." Kiera bounced out of the room, and Gertie got a kick out of how the girl wiggled her hips along the way. Hux's eyes never left the sexy young woman's backside until she was out of sight. The others were in the kitchen, cleaning up after supper, and Kiera could be heard in there schmoozing with the adults as she got the beverage.

"Hux, now that we're alone, I have one quick question for you." The old woman tapped the young man's knee. "Do you rubber up when you have sex with my great-granddaughter?"

She admired the way this Huxton Tanner quickly recovered from his gulp of surprise and manned up. "Yes, I do."

"Good boy. No need to get her pregnant yet. There will be plenty of time for that."

"Here you go." Kiera came back and handed a frothy glass to her boyfriend. "What? You both book like the cat that swallowed the goldfish. What have you been talking about?"

"Nothing, dear. We're simply enjoying each other's company." Gertie, of course, knew how to lie with the best of them. No teenager would ever have anything on her.

The evening progressed amicably, with Hank and Hux building a fire in the fieldstone fireplace. Everyone gathered in the cozy living room, enjoying the ambiance of the sanguine evening indoors while the summer rain pattered outside. Gertie loved this room with its cushy furniture and casual cottage feel. She had to admit, she'd missed it, no matter how much she insisted on being in a nursing home. She pulled the deep pink afghan she'd knitted – When? Fifty years ago? – around her legs. Wearing her favorite pale pink velour sweatsuit, although she couldn't remember the last time she'd done anything strenuous enough to make her actually sweat – she felt comfy, with the afghan topping off the feeling of being at home.

Sheer happiness, that was what she felt, she decided.

Chapter 21

When Hux came to sit beside her again, Gertie asked him what he studied in college.

"I'm getting my master's degree in history. I want to be a history professor, but I also want to research and write. I specialize in Native American, First People's, beliefs and practices. Kiera said she told you I'm part Chippewa. My grandmother was full-blooded."

Gertie watched the young man as he talked, and she liked the non-braggadocio way he described his ambitions. She liked it that her great-granddaughter would be joining with a native of this land. It felt like coming full circle from the time when she herself felt nationless, like she didn't belong in her own country during the reign of the Third Reich.

"I hope you don't mind," Hux said, "but Kiera played some your recording for me. I can't wait to hear the rest of it. I've recorded my grandparents' stories, too, and I treasure them. Especially one my grandmother did where she speaks in the old Chippewa language and then translates it."

Now Gertie liked this Hux even more. He respected his elders. So many young people had no idea how much they would benefit from taking the time to learn from their grandparents.

"Much like your grandparents', mine is a story you won't read in history books."

"Yes. That's why I want to write – rewrite – about history. I want to tell the real stories of real people. That's true history. And, you're right, that's not what we usually find."

"That's good. It's good for an old lady to know that a young person will be doing that."

"My grandmother said the same thing.

"I do have one question for you," he added thoughtfully.

Hank, Leona, and Marilyn had finished up in the kitchen and came in to join them. Without interrupting, they sat down and listened intently.

"How did a man like Hitler manage to come to power? I've never been able to figure out what made people follow him in the first place."

Gertie nodded. "You and millions of others, including me. Not that I haven't thought about it a lot over the years. At times, I've had to force myself to give it up so I could sleep at night. But I know a few things about it."

She paused to take a sip of her beer. Then, straightening her back as best she could and looking from person to person around the room, she said, "First of all, Hitler caught Germany at its weakest. They'd lost World War I, there was an economic depression, and people wanted an easy out. They were vulnerable, and Hitler was a master at taking advantage of vulnerability. He made grandiose promises." She swept out her arms in a grand gesture. "Mind you, there were a lot of good people who fell for his bullshit. He could be very charming and persuasive amidst all his bluster. Basically, we were hornswoggled.

"He was a failed artist. A loser. Insecure. His sick mind needed to be fed with constant adulation. He started out in the early 1930s by holding big events in beer halls. They were exciting. There was entertainment. People saw him as being one of them. Many considered him to be an excellent speaker, although I always thought he came off as a pompous ass. Plenty of women even thought he was sexy, which was beyond me.

She looked off into the distance of the room. "Leo and I talked about this very thing one night. How had we come to this? And how did we, he and I and all of the ordinary people we knew, get caught up in the very middle of it?"

Unterreichenbach, 1944
"Leo, what makes people follow that monster?"

They sat on the bed facing each other, smoking as usual, their legs crisscrossed like kids. Leo blew smoke toward the ceiling before answering.

"He hoodwinked us. Kidnapped an entire nation. And we let it happen." He puffed hard, his anger taken out on that small, white, cindering stick.

"From the very first, I thought he was an arrogant ass, but so are lots of politicians." Gerta's brow furrowed, belying her bewilderment. "So I didn't think much of it when he was elected. We lived in a democracy. His time would come and go. Little did I know what lay ahead."

"That he would take power and do away with our democracy." Leo had frenetically smoked his cigarette down to a stub and squashed it out in the ashtray. He patted his pocket for more, pulled out an empty pack, sighed, crushed it, and cast it away. "At first he simply broke a law here and there. Then he did away with laws that didn't serve his purposes and with government agencies that oversaw a democratic system. He was methodical, crafty, and underhanded. A real shyster. His dictatorship had overtaken our government before we as citizens even knew what hit us."

"What I've never understood is how he got so many German people to believe that we were a race of our own, better than all other races." As she spoke, Gerta handed him what was left of her cigarette, so that he could finish it off.

"That is a conundrum, isn't it?" He gestured pointedly, cigarette in hand. "At first I thought that must be a joke. How could people who lived within the borders of a country be a race unto themselves? What about people who moved over the border? Were they still part of that race? It was ridiculous. I know his thinking is more complicated than that – it has to do with physical characteristics – but basically he is saying Germans. I don't have an answer as to why anyone would believe something so absurd, but I do know it's a power-grabbing technique as old as the human race: separate someone from others in order to control them. Us versus them. If Germans were better than everyone else in the world, they didn't have anyone to listen to but der Führer himself. We do have to give him credit for being a master manipulator."

"I know, but I don't want to give him credit for anything. What truly dumbfounds me is how he got religious people to abandon their God for him. He became their God. I've known people like that in this very town. In the beginning, before we all became afraid to say anything, some of us would point out that by supporting a man so despicable, they were putting him above their God. They insisted that God loved Germans above all others, because everybody else on the planet didn't believe in Him the same way they did. So, they were superior."

"That was part of Hitler's never-ending mumbo-jumbo. Another way to manipulate people."

"They would say that God had given them Hitler, so they had to support him. When we pointed out that meant they were worshipping Hitler more than God, they would simply rationalize it away. They didn't even realize he had made himself their God. Ugh! It was so frustrating." Gerta shook her head in distress.

Chapter 22

Harbor Springs, 2015

Gertie did her best to relay the essence of the conversation she'd had with Leo, all those years ago. She didn't know if her listeners could understand, because she hardly did. But they all sat there rapt, their full attention homed in on her. Compelled to finish this cautionary tale before she bit the dust, she continued with the woeful story of how a dictator took power.

Unterreichenbach, 1944

"He used that rhetoric to turn decent, hard-working people into a blind mob who have succumbed to his ideology of entitlement and hate." Leo seethed with anger. "His bigotry is legendary, but the fact that he's been able to convince so many others of it is truly terrifying."

"I'll never understand that."

"Another draw is that his big war machine has provided lots of manufacturing jobs. Some people have enjoyed better incomes than ever before. Many still are. Especially families like mine, who are in the manufacturing business. We used to make automobile parts. Now it's all war machinery."

"Leo, how did you end up in the SS? I've always wondered."

"My uncle was an acquaintance of the Führer's because of our factories. It was my uncle who got me this relatively safe position with the SS. Better than combat fighting. At first, I tried to leave the country when I realized what was happening. But I waited too long. War started and I couldn't get out. My uncle was influential and protective, but he died a couple of years ago."

"Have you ever met Hitler?"

He nodded. "On several occasions. Mostly at social gatherings, because of my family's connections, and through the SS, of course. I've been around him enough to know he's garnered a following of fanatical supporters who slavishly surround him and protect him from dissent. They are small-minded, insignificant people who want to feel important. They want to feel like they're part of something big, like they're bigshots. He feeds their insecurities like a master feeding mangy, starving dogs."

"This might sound silly," Gerta confessed, "but when the radio stopped playing music and started playing nothing but his speeches; which are rambling, incoherent – boring! – tirades, as far as I'm concerned; and we could no longer see a decent movie, only his propaganda, I hated him on yet another level. He'd taken away so much of the joy in our lives. I couldn't understand why more people weren't furious about that. I stopped listening to the radio and don't even think about the movies. Newspapers are filled with his drivel and are shut down if they don't comply. Good books are even hard to come by. I had to hide my copies of *Madame Bovary* and *Wuthering Heights* lest Wilhelm would confiscate them. God forbid I could ever have a moment of pleasure."

"Wilhelm was your husband?"

"Unfortunately. A Nazi through and through."

"Ah, I see. Well, rest assured, Gerta, you can read whatever you want as long as I'm around." The relief from the somber thread of this conversation made her smile.

Black Forest

Harbor Springs, 2015

Gertie smiled at the memory of Leo's warmth, then cleared her throat to continue her tale. Her voice had become scratchy and she'd grown weary but would not be deterred. Her memory and mental acuity had sharpened, infused with youthful vigor in her desperate need to finish this.

"Leo said that Hitler was a genius at using the media. In fact, it was his most effective power-grabbing technique. In the end, it all amounted to 'the power of perpetual propaganda,' Leo said. For Hitler, it was always all about power, all about proving to himself and to the world that he was better than anyone else. He didn't care about the German people any more than he cared about a scroungy alley rat in the slums. He was an impudent, arrogant, narcissistic, delusional little man. A psychopath. Did I leave anything out? There aren't enough nasty English words to describe someone as cruel and callow as Adolf Hitler. He was ein verrükter, a lunatic.

"Of course, there were plenty of independent thinkers who didn't fall for his crap. But by the time people realized how malevolent the Third Reich was, and how diabolical our Führer really was, it was too late. Dissenters were hunted down and killed.

"As a nation, we were trapped. It was go along or die. It was that simple. He had kidnapped our nation and held it hostage for twelve long years.

"And, what he did to children was pure horror." Gertie took a deep breath and looked into the fire. The room filled with the ghosts of the children she had lost. "You know that story. He grew his own cult by taking children from their parents and turning them into his slaves.

"But most of all, I think people continued to follow him, no matter what, because they didn't want to face reality and wouldn't admit they had been wrong. It was pride. Stupid pride. When confronted with facts about the horrible things he had done, they would double down on their stupid decision to support their Führer." Gertie weakly pounded her fists on her lap in disgust. "The sick rationalization people must have made up in their minds in order to justify supporting that monster is mind-boggling.

"There were a lot of us who did face reality. Lots of people tried to oust him. My Leo and others like him tried."

"There was a movie a few years back," Hank interjected, "*Valkyrie*, about one group who tried to kill him with a bomb."

"Yes." Gertie nodded. "They failed. Like they all did. It's only been in the years since the war that we've learned how many attempts were made on der Führer's life. Many. But to no avail. Millions of lives had to be lost before that one asshole could be stopped."

"Rotting in hell isn't good enough for Adolf Hitler!" Leona cut in, her ire blaring. "I hope that bastard burns in hellfire until kingdom come, with his pathetic minions right beside him."

Gertie mused at her daughter's fervor and how she had gone from disinterest to loathing.

"If there is a God, Hell is where he is. But here's the important thing about Hitler's reign." Gertie pointed a gnarly finger at Marilyn, then Kiera, and then Hux. "It could happen again. You young people have to watch out. There are politicians and businessmen out there today who are like Adolf Hitler. Arrogant power mongers. Pay attention to the past. Learn from history." Her voice rose to a surprisingly strong timber. "Don't let the Third Reich reign again.

Choose your leaders wisely. Better yet, you lead, in any way you can."

The old woman took a ragged breath, leaned in, and looked up into Hux's bedazzling brown eyes. "That might have been a longer answer than you were looking for."

"It was a perfect answer. Thank you for your candor. I am honored that you have shared it with me."

Oh, Gertie thought, if only she were eighty years younger, she would be head over heels in love. She gazed up at him. It thrilled her that her great-granddaughter would get the chance for a life with a man like this, a chance that she herself never had.

Chapter 23

Harbor Springs, 2015

Kiera woke up happy. Fingering the "Hux" tattoo on her hip, the one her mother had no idea existed, she got goosebumps as she laid there languishing in the memory of last night's sex with her boyfriend in his truck. Later, after the family get-together, Hux told her he'd fallen in love with Granny Gertie. That made Kiera love him all the more.

Granny Gertie. What an enigma. It had always been obvious Granny was a strong woman, but no one in the family had had any idea how strong. Kiera couldn't imagine what she'd gone through.

During a horrendous time in a deadly, terrifying place; Gerta Gruber had remained true to herself, thinking for herself. She did not waver in the throes of the mob mentality that had made so many support a delusional dictator. Her granny had not given in.

And she had murdered her own husband! She did it to save her children, especially her son. Kiera couldn't imagine life without her great-uncle, Hank. He'd always been there; steadfast, funny, and caring.

Could she herself kill a living human being who had caused the death of three of her children and threatened the lives of her others? She shuddered at the thought. It seemed unimaginable that she would ever have to answer that question.

But... if there were no other choice?

One thing was certain: Kiera felt blessed to come from such strength. It solidified her resolve to be a strong woman herself. Live up to her potential. Take care of herself. Think for herself, even if she chose to share her life with Hux. Protect her children.

Yes... she could do it.

She slipped out of bed as quietly as possible so she wouldn't wake her mom, who soundly slept in the other twin bed. Grabbing the clothes she'd left draped over a chair, she padded out of the room and tottered down the hall to the bathroom.

Pleased with what she saw in the mirror as she washed up, she ran the events of the prior evening through her mind. The conversation had turned light after the discussion about Hitler. Everybody had laughed and laughed as Gertie's children reminded her of all the fun adventures they'd had growing up. Swimming, rock hunting, hiking, bike riding, skating, sledding, skiing, and camping in the rain – always camping in the rain, they insisted. Everything outdoor Michigan had to offer, they had enjoyed. There had been tricks played on each other, a couple of broken bones, and a mumps outbreak, but always there had been family taking care of family.

By nine o'clock, though, Granny had fallen asleep on the couch, her head on Hux's shoulder. Hank carried her to the bedroom, and the girls got her into her favorite flowered nightgown. It had been like dressing a rag doll. She didn't even wake up.

Ready to face the day, Kiera peeked into Granny's bedroom to check on her. To her surprise, the bedding was cast aside and the bed was empty.

"Granny?"

No answer. She went in and checked the en suite bathroom. Not there. The wheelchair sat folded up by the bed. Ah, that meant Uncle Hank had carried Granny somewhere. However, when Kiera passed the staircase, she could hear her great-uncle's soft snoring up in the attic bedroom. Her heart started to race. A crippled old woman couldn't have disappeared all on her own.

Kiera scrambled through the living room, tiptoeing so she wouldn't wake up Grandma Leona, who indeed slept on the couch, as she'd insisted. Kiera hurried to the kitchen. No Granny.

But on the table there was a note in unmistakable flowery cursive handwriting. A beautiful antique sapphire and diamond ring sat beside it. She picked up the ring in one hand and examined it in wonder, then picked up the note in her other hand. "My dear Kiera, this is for you, a family heirloom engagement ring from your great-grandfather. He gave it to me, passed down from his grandmother, the gypsy, and his grandfather, her husband. They all would have loved you so very much. I know I do. I hope you will wear this ring knowing that our love surrounds you every moment of every day of your life. Forever, your Granny Gertie." Kiera gently set down the note and placed the ring on her finger. It fit perfectly, as if made for her. She could have sworn that her forebears gazed down on her at this very moment, their spirits infusing themselves into her being to remind her that she came from strong stock and could handle whatever came her way in life.

"Oh, thank you. I love you, too," she whispered to all of her ancestors who had touched this marvelous ring. Anxious to thank her great-grandmother in person, she rushed outside, and sighed a big sigh of relief. There was Granny Gertie with her back to the cottage, still in her nightgown, lush white hair tussled, sitting on her garden bench facing the lake. Her cane leaned on the bench beside her. Miraculously, she'd harnessed the strength to walk out there by herself. How wonderful that she got to do something she loved so much.

Not wanting to startle her, Kiera stepped lightly down the path, taking in the beauty of the morning. Everything seemed opulent, heightened, which felt so appropriate on this the grand day when she'd received such a meaningful gift from her ancestors and her granny had been able to come out to her own beloved garden.

The out-of-doors was awash with freshness from the former night's shower. Lake Michigan glistened with early light. Wispy white clouds graced the sky. The blue, pink, white, and lavender of Granny's peonies, snapdragons, baby's breath, and forget-me-knots glowed as if emanating light. The lingering scent of rain-bathed pine and lilac mingled to fill the air with aromatic delight. It was a time and place that intensified the senses and imbued life.

"Good morning Granny dear...."

Kiera froze upon reaching Gertie's side. For what felt like an eternity, the young woman stood like an ice statue and stared.

"Oh, Granny," she finally thawed enough to whimper. "Granny Gertie. No. No, no, no."

Gently, as if touching an ethereal angel, Kiera ran a trembling hand over her great-grandmother's whimsical hair and placed a gentle kiss on her wizened forehead.

Turning back toward the cottage, Kiera took a few stumbled steps before calling out. "Mom! Grandma! Uncle Hank! Come quick!"

Within minutes the old woman's family knelt around her, each with a hand on her lifeless body. Tears flowed as they looked upon the peaceful face of Granny Gertie, one Gerta Gruber, the strong, brave woman who had not only made them, but had made them who they were.

"Look," Hank said. "She has a sprig of forget-me-knots in her hand."

"And look at her other hand," Leona noted. "It's stretched out on her lap as if she was reaching for something."

They all gazed up in the direction of that reach to be met with the garden, the lake, and the never-ending sky.

Chapter 24

Harbor Springs, 2020

"Leo! Leo! Where's my Leo?"

Of course, Kiera knew right where her two-year-old was, always keeping an eye on him the way she did. But he loved this game they played in Granny Gertie's garden each summer morning as Kiera picked fresh flowers for the cottage.

"Oh my, where could my Leo be?" She twirled around in pretend consternation.

"I here!" The toddler shrieked with glee as he popped out from behind the garden bench clapping his hands and dancing on his tippy toes, certain he'd fooled his mommy once again. He ran to her and clasped his short arms around her leg.

Kiera ruffled his jet black hair. "I love you."

"I wuv you, too."

"Here, would you like to carry these?" She pulled a sprig of pastel forget-me-knot blossoms out of the bouquet she carried and handed it to him.

"'kay." He took hold of the stems and, taking his job very seriously, stoically held them upright.

Taking his other hand, Kiera said, "How about we go inside and have breakfast with Daddy? We have some yummy cinnamon twists."

"Yay! Cin-mon twips!"

"We can come back out to Granny Gertie's garden after while."

They headed for the cottage, but Leo suddenly pulled away and ran back to the bench. "'Bye, Granny Ger-ee." Gingerly, he laid the sprig of forget-me-knots on the seat. "See you affer whi-ah! I wuv you!" He waved at the air around the garden seat and ran back to his mother, nonchalantly taking her hand again.

Stunned, Kiera stared at her son. She looked back at the bench, then back at her son. "Sweetie, she loves you, too. I'm sure of it. She loves you, too."

She glanced at the bench once again – and grinned.

Das Ende

Author's Note

Black Forest, a work of fiction, was inspired by two true stories of people I know. One is a story told by the granddaughter of a German woman who lived through the horrors of World War II, and another is a friend who escaped her war-torn German town when she was six years old.

But long before hearing those stories, my fascination with this topic started when I was a high school senior a hundred years ago – okay, it was 1966 – and I was offered an opportunity to do a project rather than attend world history class. It had something to do with skipping school a lot and that being my only opportunity to graduate. Anyway, I chose to research and write about Adolf Hitler and the Third Reich. I don't recall what on earth made me, a seventeen-year-old girl, want to delve into the historical relevance of the life of a despicable dictator.

I started my research by reading *The Rise and Fall of the Third Reich: A History of Nazi Germany,* by William L. Shirer. I reported on that and other resources, and received a B+ for the project, which disappointed me mightily. That had been some tough reading. But one of the conditions was that I do college-level work. The teacher said it was not perfect at a college level.

Many, many years later, when I was a college professor (so there, high school teacher!), and was also doing public memoir writing workshops, I always suggested to students and to writers that they interview any elders they may have in their families. Often, they came away shocked by what they learned. Stories that would never be told to children, rightfully so, were revealed once those children grew up. I have never forgotten those tales, including the one about the German mother who had to turn to prostitution for the Nazis after her husband died and she was left with many children to feed.

Another real-life story that impacted me came from Ingrid Bloom, who told about escaping with her family from her hometown of Dresden, Germany, just before it was bombed and destroyed by the Allies. Her mother remained a Hitler supporter all of her life. Ingrid, however, grew up to move to America, and fall in love with and marry a Jewish Rabbi. (Can you imagine those family gatherings?!) Find Ingrid's story of the joy she found in her adult life in our book *What We Talk about When We're Over Sixty*, a collection of women's stories.

Research fleshed out the rest of *Black Forest*. The revelations about how children were treated by the Third Reich shattered my heart. I didn't include all of that here, but good resources are readily available if you want to learn more, including the memoirs *Flakhelfer to Grenadier: Memoir of a Boy Soldier, 1943-1945*, by Karl Heinz Schleisier, and *Twenty-three Years: Childhood, War, Escape*, by Eve Monk. There are a plethora of other resources about the history of Nazi Germany.

A burning question that haunts me still is: what made everyday people believe in, rabidly support, and slavishly follow a madman like Adolf Hitler? There are many speculations in my book, but I don't know that anyone has a single definitive answer.

Obviously, the civil unrest we are experiencing in our country in this year of 2020 has dredged up these questions in my mind, long buried just beneath the surface. It has caused me to become compelled to write this story, which feels as if it's been haunting me ever since I was that seventeen-year-old girl.

Have we learned anything from the history of the Third Reich? Or is it already being repeated? What are your thoughts?

Essentially, this is a story about how we must never let the darkness of evil prevail. There are many ways out of the darkness, many shades of hope. The light is always there, even when it seems as if we're lost in the forest during what feels like the never-ending black of night. The sun always rises, and we will once again know the power of its light if we raise our sights and look up into the promise of an everlasting sky.

Next in the *Shades of Hope Novella Collection*:
Gold Mountain
There might be gold in them thar hills, but curmudgeonly San Francisco business tycoon Caden Caldwell is searching for his son, Colt, to try to rein in the wild young man. What he finds instead is something else altogether: orphaned children, wayward women, and an Alaskan town full of quirky panhandlers. He knows how to manage big city business, but what on earth is he supposed to do when he becomes isolated in the dead of winter with this motley crew?

Will he ever be the same? Does he even want to be?

Go back to 1896 and join Caden Caldwell on Gold Mountain. You might strike gold, after all.

Other Novels by Linda Hughes:
Secrets of the Asylum
Secrets of the Island
Secrets of the Summer
Tough Rocks
The House on Haven Island
Becoming Jessie Belle
Homecoming Queen
Fountain Street Heat

Where to Find Linda:
Amazon author page: amazon.com/author/lindagayhughes
Website: www.lindahughes.com
Facebook: /lindahughesauthor
Twitter: @lghughesauthor
Instagram: /lghughesauthor
Pinterest: /lghughesauthor

Made in the USA
Columbia, SC
21 November 2020